Dennis E. R... (handwritten signature)

D0430722

2710 So. Academy #139
Colorado Springs
xxx-7667

San Carves the Beast

San adjusted quickly to Pegleg's flash. He darted forward, his curved knife in his left hand. Two slingmen followed him, knives glittering. They pounced on the great coils with their horny feet, holding down the front end of the creature while San's knife probed and ripped under the scales behind the mutilated head. In a moment the head sagged, although the yards of heavy body behind it kept up an uncoordinated lashing. This soon changed to a series of shudders, and then the thing lay still.

San looked coldly at the thick, dark blue blood on his knife, and at the long heavy cylinder of the monster's body. In the smashed head, imposing rows of sharp teeth showed.

"*Attar!*" San said. "*Volloon attar!*"

By the Same Author

STARDUST VOYAGES

The Ramsgate Paradox

Stephen Tall

A BERKLEY MEDALLION BOOK
published by
BERKLEY PUBLISHING CORPORATION

For Leslie and Steve and Judy
(since this is usually the order in which they read Dad's stories)

Copyright © 1976, by Crompton N. Crook

All rights reserved

Published by arrangement with the author's agent.

All rights reserved which includes the right
to reproduce this book or portions thereof in
any form whatsoever. For information address

Lurton Blassingame
60 East 42nd Street
New York, N.Y. 10017

SBN 425-03186-0

BERKLEY MEDALLION BOOKS are published by
Berkley Publishing Corporation
200 Madison Avenue
New York, N.Y. 10016

BERKLEY MEDALLION BOOK ® TM 757,375

Printed in the United States of America

Part I

The Slingmen of Hadorn

Chapter 1

The planet lay beneath us. We had matched orbital speed with its speed of rotation and so hung poised, without apparent progress, a thousand miles above the planet's surface. Cameras were recording in our usual meticulous fashion. All our electronic sensors were operating, collating all energy emissions from the world below, synthesizing, analyzing. Before we go down, we know what to expect, what we're up against. I think we do a good job.

There's a place on the side of the *Stardust* where, when the time and conditions are right, plates of the impervious skin of the starship slide smoothly back and a transparent blister extrudes. In this blister, surrounded on three sides by space, Ursula Potts sits at her easel and paints. When a planet is being analyzed from orbit, the little transparent studio is always out.

Among our highly trained personnel and sophisticated equipment, Ursula Potts is an enigma. The Earth calendar above my desk said 2127, but Ursula looks like 1915. With her witch's face, strange pale eyes, great bun of gray hair on the back of her head, and skinny clawlike hands, Ursula would have been at home in anybody's nightmares.

Still, we could have done without a lot of the complicated analytical equipment, if we'd had to. But we had come to depend on Ursula. Those strange eyes saw the truth, and those skinny hands put it on canvas with a weird and uncanny genius.

"Something screwy, Roscoe."

Ursula's painting didn't look like our view of the planet below. But that wasn't unusual. Often they don't. The paintings are Ursula's interpretation of the situation.

3

"Looks good to me."

From a thousand miles we could see a sizable stretch of the planet's curved surface. Practiced eyes could pick up mountain ranges, high and rugged, forest land, plains, extensive water. Zoom lenses showed vegetation variety. Spectroscopes had verified an oxygen-rich atmosphere.

Ursula's painting implied these things. It still looked funny, though.

"Color," Ursula said.

Then I got it. I realized why the painting looked queer. It was blue. All blue. Sure, there were many shades, many intensities, but that's all they were. Only one color. An ancient painter, Maxfield Parrish, would have flipped over it. But to me, when I looked closely, it was strangely depressing.

"*I* see colors," I protested.

I did, too. The planet glowed with color. Almost more than was usual from this distance. Snow-capped peaks, the stretches of water, and particularly the cloud masses blazed with yellows and oranges, violets and scarlets.

"Just it," Ursula said. "They're all here. None down there."

"How can you tell?" I didn't challenge her. By now I knew not to.

Ursula turned her pale eyes on me.

"Feel it," she said. "Way it's got to be. Don't know why."

"Kind of tosses it back in our laps, doesn't it?" I said. "It's up to us to find out. Right?"

"Always is," Ursula said.

That was so, too. Ursula's job was to paint; we, the researchers, did the investigating. Me, ecologist; Pegleg Williams, geologist; my gorgeous wife Lindy, microbiologist; Jim Peters, animal biologist; Winkie Heffelfinger, botanist; and so on. Sometimes it was hard to say just what kinds of scientists were needed on some of the problems we faced. Certainly botanist, zoologist, and the like frequently weren't very meaningful.

I took a last look at Ursula's painting, slid back the door to the lock beyond the blister. Ursula's voice stopped me.

"Roscoe," she said, "it's not as simple as it looks."

She scarcely looked my way and went back to her work almost as if I weren't there. But, for some reason, I felt a small chill as I stepped through the door.

"Dr. Kissinger! Dr. Kissinger!" An intercom outlet was whispering from the corridor wall near my ear. "Dr. Rasmussen calling Dr. Kissinger. Where're you hiding, Roscoc?"

I punched the button.

"Roscoe here, Johnny."

"Want to come to Main? We'll be dropping in before long. Do you know where you'd like to go first?"

"On my way, Johnny."

Dr. Johannes Rasmussen was the last character you'd ever choose to command a starship. Tall, lean, courtly, precise, he wore waxed moustaches and dressed for dinner even when he ate alone, which he did fairly often. Fluent in many tongues, he spoke clipped English unless his listener just plain couldn't understand it. Make no mistake about it, though: Johnny ran the *Stardust*.

There were luxury seats in Main Observation. The ten big viewscreens could be controlled from any chair. Cap'n Jules Griffin sat at ease in one, enjoying one of Johnny's cigars, saying nothing. He didn't care where we landed. To him the ship was the only reality. Pegleg Williams also had a cigar. The screen nearest him featured a snow-capped range. He was scanning it lovingly. He'd want rough country.

Moe Cheng, navigator and mapping chief, conferred with Rasmussen before a screen that showed the full sweep of the terrain below us. With slanted eyes and a nose that could never be overlooked, Moe looked like both his names. He can probably get more out of a map than any man in the galaxy.

"Cigar, Roscoe?" Pegleg invited. "They're Cuban, and free. Last chance. If you smoke down below, you'll probably blow up. High oxygen."

I had one. Then we settled down, the five of us, and went over plans. Usually we structured the drop-in together. Rasmussen had no real staff, as such. He kept things fluid. But geology, ecology, terrain, and logistics were always key considerations. Any one of us could have taken over for Johnny, if things ever called for it. So far there had never been a need.

Moe Cheng was concerned, as always, with differences, inconsistencies, in the view on the wide screen.

"Not just inhabited," he said now. "Populated. The same scars show again and again."

"Primitive," I said. "Nuts, roots, and grass stems. No industry, no cities, no roads."

"Don't jump to your usual conclusions, Roscoe," Pegleg advised. "Remember Methane II."

We remembered, all right. The only time we ever had had to break the International Space Council edict and interfere on a planet. It had looked more deserted than this, and we had seen ten million fighting "men." They weren't men, of course. They were sinuous, graceful humanoids, with a technology some aspects of which approached our own, and fatalistic Oriental ethics. They had left the surface of the planet to the lesser life-forms. Their entire complex society was under the planet's crust.

"These are topside," I said. "The scars show that. The thing that bugs me doesn't show on these screens. It's Ursula." I left it like that.

"What has Miss Potts to do with this drop-in, Dr. Kissinger?" Rasmussen spoke formally, which meant that I had caught his attention.

"Her paintings," I said. "They're all blue."

Rasmussen raised his eyebrows. His long fingers manipulated his cigar.

"Really?" he said. He stroked his moustache. "Significant," he admitted.

"Maybe Ursula's creating a new art form," said Pegleg Williams.

"She has never been entirely wrong," Moe Cheng said.

"This time, what would she be wrong about?" Pegleg flexed his plastic knee-joint. He always says it feels stiff after he sits awhile. "Any fool can see that the planet isn't blue. There's plenty of color. She's painting mood again."

"She says not. Down on the surface, the only color is blue. That's what the lady says."

"Perhaps," Johnny Rasmussen almost mused, in the dreamy deceiving way he sometimes uses, "perhaps we should call in Dr. Julio."

Phil Julio is our most profound physicist. He's especially sharp on light. I never know what he's talking about.

"He'll get on it soon enough," Pegleg said. "If we come down in a blue world, doubtless he'll notice."

We grinned. We like simple jokes. And Julio can get so wrapped up in his thoughts that he won't recognize you in the corridor.

We decided on a wide coastal plain, with a rugged, snow-capped range behind it for backdrop, and a whole complex of bays and inlets where the ocean met the land. This gave us a sweep as far as visibility was concerned. It also was ideal for towns or cities or whatever arrangement the concentrations of dominant life-forms might take.

I should explain. We never looked for men, of course. We'd never found any, and there was no reason why we should—and every reason why we shouldn't. Only the *Stardust* had Ultraspan.

As far as any evidence can show, man is an Earth species, period. And man left his planet for the first time in 1968 A.D., Earth calendar. Just one hundred fifty-nine years ago. But for the amazing development of Ultraspan we would hardly have been out of the Solar System yet. As we now know, the inhabitable planet closest to Earth is thirteen light-years from Sol. The third planet in the Primrose system isn't very Earthlike, but man can live there. We did. Four Earth weeks, Nineteen Primrose III days. And the life we found was so un-Earthlike that nothing we've found since has surprised us completely.

Primrose III taught me several things. Life is life, wherever it can be demonstrated, but the forms it can take are limitless. Ecological basics pretty much pertain. I have found four different processes that are in effect photosynthesis, but every life system we know has to trap energy from the planet's primary in some fashion.

We have since found humanoid forms, some quite advanced, and some interesting and baffling technologies. The energy systems of the disappearing cubes of Cyrene IV are as much a mystery to us now as they were when we dropped in on the planet ten years ago. But the lettucelike plant covering had chlorophyll.

I suppose you can't speak of parallel evolution in life systems of different origins. Still, there *are* humanoids. But a human culture—a human colony—would have had to come from Earth. And there just hasn't been time.

We checked and alerted all personnel, retracted Ursula's blister, and then the *Stardust* began its long glide down into the atmosphere, through scattered layers and patches of clouds. There was no appreciable friction, no heat, no speed buildup. We were past all that. If Rasmussen had ordered it, Cap'n Jules could have brought us in at ten miles an hour, as smooth as a piece of thistledown coming down a sunbeam.

The thousand miles became ten miles, the ten miles five thousand feet. The mountaintops in the distance reached high above us, vegetation spread and diversified below us. And everything was blue.

Blue is cold. Even the most subtle shades seem to drain away warmth. Blue beauty is stark, metallic, forbidding. This land, this planet, was all of that.

Johnny Rasmussen directed from Main, though Cap'n Jules had gone back to Control. The great ship swung over the plain in a hundred-mile circle, and finally set down into what looked like a field of grain. Blue grain.

The atmosphere had been continually scooped and analyzed as we came in. There was no detectable reason why it shouldn't be completely breathable. High oxygen, as Pegleg had said, but only about twenty-six percent. That would just keep us feeling zippy.

Still, we sat in Main awhile and discussed, while the stuff was being pumped into chambers of small animals, their reactions noted and their blood analyzed. Lindy and her lab associates sorted out the microspecimens. If there were any micro-menaces, we'd be notified. Contrary to what you might suspect, we had rarely had trouble from such sources.

"I like things different," Pegleg Williams said, "but this is ridiculous. The spectrum is the spectrum. There ought to be color in variety out there, but even the sun is blue."

"The explanation, I suppose, is simple enough," I said. "A belt of something is reflecting or absorbing all light except blue wavelengths. What, how, why, actually do not concern me much. Phil Julio can throw off sparks about that."

"We should have detected the reason coming in," Moc Cheng said. "Matter of fact, we probably did. When the energy data are analyzed, I imagine it'll show up."

"Nothing to it," Pegleg said sourly. "No reason at all why we shouldn't run into a blue world once in a while. Or maybe a nice red one. Polka-dot, I suppose, would be harder."

Pegleg is my buddy in the field. He's an instinctive, great geologist. But he's also a narrow-faced, cross-grained, often sour human being, occasionally gracious, always verbose.

"What do you care?" I said now. "Rocks is rocks. They're hard and dead and uninteresting. If they're all blue, you at least have a small challenge there."

"As soon as Johnny gives the word, I'm going to have a look," Pegleg said. "You may join me, if you feel like working. You can scrape blue lichens off of my blue rocks."

"I'll just go walkabout in the neighborhood," I decided. "The *Stardust* is bedded down in somebody's wheatfield, if you haven't noticed. He'll probably be around asking how come. A fifteen-hundred-foot ship will cut his profits some, I'd say."

"Is that your considered opinion, Roscoe?" Rasmussen asked. "That this is not wild natural growth?"

The big screens of Main were like windows. The sea of grass waved around us, five or six feet tall, neatly spaced, sweeping away for some miles in all directions. One species, a clear stand. Heavy fruiting heads were beginning to bow the top of each stalk.

"If it is," I said, "Mother Nature is doing a better-than-usual job, Johnny. And if you're wondering about the life that belongs to this grange organization, I'm right with you. I'm wondering, too."

"There was a scar ahead as we came in," Moe Cheng spoke from his viewscreen. "One of those we associated with advanced life concentrations."

"If you mean 'town,' why don't you say 'town'?" Pegleg broke in.

Cheng grinned. "Because I don't necessarily mean town," he said. "I don't know what I mean. But the scars are artificial. Something made them. Closeup pics will probably show shelters, buildings, roads. That would be a life concentration, wouldn't it?"

"It would be a town," Pegleg said. "Probably with cinemas, nightclubs, and blue dancing-girls."

Sometimes it helps to remember that today's men are only yesterday's little boys. And that some make the transition more completely than others.

You may wonder why we sat at ease, wrangling and making with random talk, when we had just dropped in on an unknown, uncharted world, a world the eye of man had never seen. Well, we were veterans. We had done this before. We weren't unexcited; we just knew what the procedure had to be.

We had to have assurance that the outside was habitable for us. The experts in atmosphere, radiation, microbiology, all were busy at their specialties. Actually, we were waiting for "all-clear." I remembered an ancient baseball catcher's remark about high pop fouls behind the plate. "You can't never catch one of them things until it comes down." We were waiting for it to come down.

Lindy came into the lounge, and every man instantly and instinctively stood up. It's something a man can scarcely help.

She's the first thing I see, the first thing I look for, when I open my eyes in the morning. If she's not yet awake, I often lie propped on an elbow and study her; study the clean graceful planes of her face, the perfect, glowing skin, the red curls tumbled over the pillow. Sometimes covered, sometimes not, the sweet curves and breathtaking emphases of her lithe body are things I never get used to. I never dream of the Ultimate Allure, the final female perfection, the Galactic Queen of Love and Beauty; I don't have to. She's lying there in my bed.

"Reporting, Dr. Rasmussen," Lindy said demurely, but

her green eyes were anything but. "All indicated studies have been made. If the planet isn't habitable for us, it's due to something we haven't anticipated." She winked at me and added, "And *do* sit down, gentlemen!"

"Thank you, Dr. Peterson." Rasmussen only occasionally remembers that Lindy's name is Kissinger now, and has been for ten years.

He turned to us. "First investigative phase now in effect," he said formally. "Two days free reconnaissance. We will meet in seventy-two hours—all section chiefs and investigative heads—and plan a pattern. You're on your own, gentlemen. I will notify Mr. Price."

Stony Price is communications chief. He would put the orders on intercom, and the entire *Stardust* personnel would go into an activity pattern as structured as a fire drill or an abandon-ship alert. Each individual knew his job. Then at the planning meeting he'd report as an expert. We got results because we were the best. The chief knew it and depended on it. That's why he, too, was the best.

Lindy came across the lounge and slipped a hand into mine.

"I want to go, Roscoe," she said.

"Go where?"

"I've no idea," my wife said. "Who can tell what you're thinking? But you're going somewhere—and I want to go."

"It sounds like a good offer," I said. "Where to, Pegleg?"

"The foothills," Pegleg said. "I'll take a jumper. The jeep would mess up that grain out there, and I've got a sort of feeling that that wouldn't be good public relations."

"Hum-m. Spoil your chances with the blue dancing-girls." I considered. "I think I'll just opt for the neighborhood, as I said. Maybe circle the grainfield. Knowing nothing about what has developed in and adapted to that blue light, one place will be as good as another for me."

"I'm dying to get out in it," Lindy said.

"That's an awkward way to put it, Dr. Peterson," I said. "You have much to live for."

"Sorry, sir," my wife said. "How do we dress?"

"Field regular," I decided. "We'd better take jumpers too. Pegleg's right about the grain. The less we damage it the better."

At need the *Stardust* could extrude jumper platforms along its sides, open intricate shutterlike ports through which the scoutboats could be launched, or just slide back regular ports for freight, supplies, or personnel. From outside they were undetectable. In fact, when we chose to make it so, the *Stardust* could become completely featureless. From afar it looked more like a giant sausage than anything else, always lying inertly at full length. In this light—well, face it: in this light it was probably blue.

Chapter 2

Air temperature, 74 degrees Fahrenheit. Position of primary, almost at zenith. Wind gentle, just rippling the heavy heads of the grain. Lindy and I stood on our jumper platform forty feet above the land, and stared about us in as near astonishment as we ever come. Being outside *did* make a difference.

But for the foothills in the near distance and the farther, rugged, looming range, it was like blue Kansas. From the ship the coarse blue grass rolled away, miles of it. If there was a settlement near, it was beyond our view. We knew that the coastline was not far away, but there was no hint of it here.

"Roscoe!" There was panic in Lindy's voice. I turned. She was staring at me in horror.

I had been so interested in the view that I had not consciously looked at Lindy. I did now. For a minute it got me, too, but then I knew what ailed her.

"Take it easy, Dr. Peterson," I said. "Don't forget your physics—you know, the section on light."

My wife was a horrible cadaver blue. Her beautiful crisply curling auburn ringlets were a dead charcoal gray. Her red lips were black, and her eyes were almost colorless pools in that blue face. Her red jerkin-blouse was as black as her lips, her short green skirt only a little less blue-black. She looked like she had just left her tomb for a brief constitutional.

Now, I'm not beautiful like Lindy. I'm wide—heavy-shouldered, thick-armed, pillar-legged—with a chest that's a mat of black hair, and no hair at all on my head. What the local illumination was doing with that you can probably imagine. For under the best of conditions I can only assume that Lindy is in love with my kindly soul; it can't be anything she can see.

13

She adjusted promptly. Within a few minutes she was giggling.

"What you look like, Roscoe, I'll write in my diary, but I'll never, never tell you!"

"Just as well," I said. My grin probably showed blue teeth. "Flattery would spoil me for work. First stop the knoll over there, where the grain is thin. Follow me!"

My jumper launched in a high arc, cutting off at the peak, and dropping me gently into the grain fifty yards from the ship. On impact it blasted again, and I took another kangaroo leap. I stood loosely in the frame, taking advantage of the momentary altitude to look about in all directions. Lindy's jumper tapped and soared behind me. Eight jumps—four hundred yards—brought us to the little hillock that stood well above the level of the rolling grain field. We cut power and surveyed.

Even at that distance, the prone bulk of the *Stardust* was an alien and awesome thing, or at least it must have seemed so to any native observers. To us, of course, it was home. Just to see it lying there gave a warm feeling in this strange blue light.

Whap!

I sensed, rather than saw, the hurtling stone. It cracked into the soil between our jumpers, bounding away into the grain.

"Forcefield!"

I flipped my own switch. Lindy was as prompt. There was no visible change around us, but within the minute the difference was demonstrated. The next stone was on target. Without the forcefield it would have got me just about the middle of the belly. Instead, it ricocheted as though it had hit a glass wall. It had come in on a low trajectory, a water-worn, rounded rock almost the size of a baseball.

There was a low, piercing yell, a strange keening, as the rock bounced away. Half a dozen tall, thin men were circling us in the grain. They must have been reconnoitering the ship and have flattened as we came leaping across with our jet-propelled giant jumps.

"Men" is correct. It didn't seem reasonable that they *could* be anything else. Much taller, much longer, far thinner than the black Masai of Earth's Africa, they were swift, darting, agile runners, always changing position. Using slings, they tried the rock gambit again.

Three rocks bounded from my forcefield, three from Lindy's, and one of hers glanced onto me and bounded a second time. The keening came again. It told of bafflement and astonishment. Later we learned that that single incident established our image for all time here. For the slingmen of Hadorn were the most deadly marksmen of any primitives we ever encountered or heard of. How that first stone missed I'll never know, unless it was meant to. That our bodies turned their stones was unbelievable to them: nothing else in their world could withstand those projectiles.

Men! Not humanoids! I felt my own subconscious denying this with irritation. They couldn't be human. There hadn't been time! Even a glance could verify that these men and this environment had been together for a long, long time. For millennia. So they couldn't be men—yet I knew they were.

They formed into a little group about a hundred yards from us. The low, sharp murmur of conference came to us. Strange, thin, long, almost naked creatures, but men. I guessed their height at close to eight feet. Every body feature and structure was elongated. I put a glass on them. Smooth, long, hairless heads, slanted slits of eyes, long noses, thin-lipped mouths. A belt and a breech covering. A recognizable knife at each hip. A large lumpy pouch or bag depended from each belt, and we soon saw what that was for: it was the ammo bag.

They tried the sling bit one more time. Or one did. He stepped out from his fellows, the tallest of all. He deliberately selected a stone from his bag and slipped it into the pliant sling with an almost sleight-of-hand motion. His skeletal arm added a yard to the sling's length as he swung. One swing, and the stone came at me like a slug from a deer rifle. It would have hit me fairly between the eyes. Instead it bounded high in the air, and the moan of astonishment came again.

In many brushes with all kinds of life-forms, I had at least learned one thing: conciliation beats combat—or at least it leaves the door open. We weren't hurt. We were invaders, and they were simply doing what came naturally.

So I raised both arms, held out my empty hands, and made
what I hoped were peaceful motions. Lindy imitated me.
Even to them, she must have been a more reassuring sight
than I was. I smiled and she smiled, but the long strange faces
of the blue slingmen never changed; though they did whip
their slings around their right forearms. I assumed that it was
like shoving a six-gun back into the holster.

But they weren't finished; they just changed tactics. The
group broke up again. The men swiftly deployed around us in
a wide circle. They must have figured we couldn't watch
every direction at once. Lindy and I swung our jumper frames
back to back.

"Watch your men carefully," I directed. "They may be
going to try to rush us."

My belt communicator crackled, and the voice of Stony
Price murmured in my ear. "There's a laser on each man,"
he said. "Do you want us to do anything?"

I chuckled. I had forgotten—and the slingmen could not
possibly imagine—the complicated life-complex that lay
behind the featureless massif that was the *Stardust*. They
couldn't even guess what it was. They may not have been
able to grasp that we had come from it. We were putting on a
performance, no less, and more than four hundred people had
grandstand seats.

"Thanks, Stony," I said. "Let 'em be. They can't hurt us.
But if you could throw a baseball like they throw rocks, you
could be the pride of the American League, my friend."

What they would have done next I don't know, for the
scene changed.

The blue men saw them before I did. The wailing calls
apparently alerted all hands. Slings snapped from forearms.
The men were no longer watching us.

In the distance it looked like a flock of birds, a wheeling,
darting cluster of blue specks that rapidly grew larger. There
was a definite formation. The whirling cluster deployed into a
streamer, a ribbon of wide-winged creatures that swept down
on our sector of the grainfield and settled into it like an
infestation of five-foot starlings.

But not all settled gracefully. The long bodies of the

slingmen were whipping like catapults, and they rarely missed. When a stone struck, the creature staggered in midair, then came floundering and fluttering downward to crash into the ground. The sea of grain soon was vibrating wildly from the death throes of stricken "birds."

Those that were unhurt created even greater havoc. I've never seen more voracious eaters. Actually, they looked only vaguely like birds. But their blue-crested heads were long and bony, the extended beaklike mouths glistened with teeth, the membranous, hairy wings were held high above their woolly blue bodies as they fed. They stood as high as the plants, on long, bony blue legs. Holding their heads sideways, each pair of jaws snapped off the unripe heads of grain with the remorseless precision of a harvesting machine.

There might have been a hundred of them. The deadly slings of the blue men probably accounted for twenty. But those that landed safely now ate as if they were all alone on the planet. And the men changed tactics.

Slings wrapped again on right forearms, they moved in on the feeding "birds." Each left hand had drawn the knife, which appeared thin, blue, keen and curved. It looked vicious. As the men approached the creatures backed away, waving the great wings, watching with gimlety blue eyes. But they never stopped eating.

The men were careful. Apparently those jaws could shear off more than grain. I watched the tallest blue man, he who had taken the last shot at me. Somehow I had the impression that he gave orders and led the group. He made the first contact.

He moved in fast on the bird he had chosen. The creature raised its wings high. The man feinted with his sling-wrapped right arm. The bird struck forward with its wing-butts, like a flogging gander, and I could see that a curved, wicked-looking talon projected there. But the man wasn't touched. He swayed back. His knife flickered as it ripped the membranes of the spread wings. The creature screamed, lost its poise, and began to thrash wildly. It turned and tried to run. The flashing knife decapitated it.

That was the pattern. The men performed with a precision

that was beautiful to watch. They were never touched, but each kill took time. And all the while the remainder of the flock was destroying grain at a sinful rate. I began to understand why we had drawn such active attention from the slingmen. That grain was evidently pretty important to them.

I unclipped my laser gun, set it at lowest charge, but on wide beam. Then I deactivated my forcefield. I had an idea.

"Stay put," I said to Lindy. "Here's where I win friends and influence people."

The wide cylinder of light lanced across the grain. The creature at the end of it shriveled into a smoking mass. Its wings curled up and charred like those of a moth in a flame. shifted to another, and a third. I got a little grain, but generally I was on target. Short pulses did the trick.

I think I could have killed every bird and the slingmen would have stood their ground. It was the ray itself that got them. For it was light. Complete light. On high charge it would not have been visible, but would have messed up the scenery considerably. But this way they could see it—and it appalled them. Up to this minute, so far as I knew, they had known only blue light. This brilliant cylinder with its rainbow edges was too much.

They didn't run. Each man turned his back, shielded his eyes with his long, folded arms, and stood motionless. Apparently the posture was not only protective, but fatalistic. Each evidently expected the searing light to serve him, in his turn, as it had the birds. They awaited their fates, immobile, frozen.

But the birds were different. Obviously of a low order of intelligence, the light panicked them. Those not yet touched scrambled frantically. The wide wings beat as they exploded into terrified flight. I stopped shooting.

Actually, I had broken the basic regulation by which the *Stardust* operates by interfering at all. Legally, I could have defended myself against the slingmen, for they had attacked us. The birds hadn't. In a way, they had relieved the pressure the men were putting on us. But an attack on the birds seemed the best defense against the men, for evidently this was a familiar and a continuing struggle. I reasoned that we should be on the right side.

The wing whistles of the departing birds receded fast. For a moment we all stood, not moving, a neat little tableau for the audience in the space ship.

"Well played!" Lindy said behind me. "Bravo! Now all you've got to do is convince Johnny you don't belong in the brig. Those poor varmints weren't bothering you."

She had left her jumper frame and the safety of her forcefield.

"You're getting confidence from somewhere," I said. "Don't you realize you're the only woman I've got? Get back to your forcefield—please!" I added. Women are sensitive about these little things.

"I appreciate your concern," my wife said. "No danger now, though, I think. It was dirty pool, but you've made your point with the living skeletons. They won't throw any more rocks."

The men had not moved. I took a chance. I walked up to the nearest one, the tall one, and slapped him lightly on the back. His skin was cool and dry. At my touch he shuddered.

"Okay, pal," I said. "We be of one blood, ye and I, and like that. We're just tourists. We wouldn't harm a hair of your head—if your head had hair."

I stepped back a couple of paces. Lindy ranged alongside me, but with space between us. She was confident, but I noticed that she had a hand on her own gun.

"With dialogue like that," she said, "any court in the land would clear him if he smacked you bowlegged."

"It's a sensitive subject," I said delicately, "but I'm *already* a bit inclined in that direction. If he slapped me straight, now"—I was watching the men closely. I remembered how fast they could move.

As it happened, it was needless precaution. The man I had touched slowly lowered his arms, slowly turned to face us. Strange, blue, elongated, still there was about him an impressive dignity. He towered two feet above me. His skeletal arms and legs were well sheathed with stringy muscle. His long face remained expressionless. His cold, slanted eyes saw everything, I felt sure.

I went on with my charade. "Friend," I said. Slowly I extended my empty right hand. He stared bleakly, but made no move. Very deliberately I turned toward Lindy.

"Friend," I said.

Solemnly we shook hands.

Again I extended the hand toward the blue slingman.

"Friend," I said.

His face still didn't change, but you could see him working on it. The rocks that bounced off us, the searing light that crisped up the birds—he was touching all the bases. Then his long right arm, with the sling wrapped around it, snaked warily out. Lightly I grasped the long fingers.

"Friend," I said.

His slant eyes narrowed even more; his thin lips parted slightly. Then he got it out, in a thin, high voice.

"F'iend," he said.

It was really a good try. He surprised us by following up, too. He turned to Lindy, put out the hand. She took it and she smiled. That should have affected even a blue slingman. But not a flicker crossed his bony features.

"F'iend," he said. And Lindy echoed "Friend!"

Then we all stood, until Lindy said, "What do you do now? Invite him to tea?"

"It's his move," I said. "He'll think of something."

He did. He spoke a few syllables in his strange, high voice. His companions dropped their arms, turned to face us, five more cold, expressionless blue faces. But as I had suspected, he gave the orders. He spoke further, demonstrated. Then we each had to shake blue hands and say "Friend" five more times.

"Now," I said to Lindy, "we will turn our backs, walk slowly back to our frames, wave in a friendly fashion, and take off for the edge of the field, which seems to lie some miles over thataway, toward the hills."

We got away with it. Nothing happened. And when we waved, the tall leader extended a bony arm in answer. We could hear him speak, then five more long arms went up. I launched my jumper. Lindy followed. At the peak of each bound, as far as I could see them, the little knot of men stood there, watching, completely oblivious of the dark mass of the *Stardust* behind them, from which they were being photo-graphed, analyzed, and their very metabolism monitored.

My communicator crackled. "There is some question about your tactics," Stony Price said, "but all hands agree that the dominant species is impressed with you."

"They're my good buddies," I said. "What are they doing now, Stony?"

"Headed for home. They're so thin they can practically weave between the grass stems. Apparently they don't associate you with the ship."

"They will," I said. "They'll think it over. They're intelligent. *Really* intelligent."

"I've alerted Dr. Williams. He's the only other jumper out. Several scoutboats are cruising, but Dr. Rasmussen feels that they can't be damaged by rocks."

I chuckled, thanked Stony, and punched the *out* button.

The grain ended abruptly where the terrain rose and became rocky. Brushy growth crowded the edge of the vast field. Beyond the brush, blue forest showed shadowy and cold. There was life. Small things scuttled and hid in the brush. Winged forms, varied but all small, and looking even less like birds than the wide-winged grain eaters, perched and watched us with cold blue points of eyes, or zipped away when we came near.

"It's busy, it's varied, it's the sort of setup you like," Lindy said. "But, darn it, it just isn't cheery!"

"Mood Indigo," I agreed. "It's getting me, too. We'll go toward the suspected location of the settlement and see if we can get a distant look. We won't visit, though. Just take a peek, then go home and plan. How did the primitive slingmen plant all this wheat, for instance? Are these really the dominant species at all? Et cetera. Keep your forcefield up. There are probably squads of slingmen all around this field."

We tapped and soared, tapped and soared. A jumper will take you a mile every two minutes if you jump it flat, or it will bounce you high if you want to look around, but that cuts your linear distance.

If it hadn't been for the stream, I think we'd have missed the settlement entirely. Stream was correct enough;

"river" was better. It was a good jumper-leap wide, with a smooth current, and as you can imagine, the Blue Danube was never as blue. It made my teeth chatter just to look at it.

The grainfield ran almost to it. It didn't continue on the other side, though. There was a wide belt of trees on the far bank, huge trees, sparse of branch, and what there were growing from the upper half of the trunks. The lower boles glittered almost like metallic columns, and between them, sometimes anchored to them or even surrounding their bases, were the shelters of the blue slingmen.

"Pegleg will be disappointed," I said. "Cinemas and nightclubs seem pretty unlikely in that setup."

"No blue dancing-girls," Lindy said. "That's what will really hurt."

We were studying the settlement from the vantage of a good-sized rock outcrop a quarter of a mile from the river. We had come in flat. I doubted if we had been seen. With glasses, we had all the view we needed.

Boats were on the river, slender, pointed, needlelike boats, and the long bodies of the blue men were ideal for paddling. When we knew what to look for, we could see crude docks and wharves. Both logs and stone had been used. And the more I looked, the more Earthlike everything appeared.

"Take away the blue light," I said, "and that would look amazingly homelike."

"Your home, not mine," my wife said maliciously. "So you really did grow up in a thatched hut, after all!"

"After dinner, with brandy at elbow, I will remember to be insulted," I said. "It's Earthlike, doll! The slingmen are human. Earth-human. There isn't any other kind."

Lindy gave me a ghastly black-lipped smile.

"You're trying too hard, Roscoe," she said gently. "You were bound to run into it sooner or later. Duplicate as well as parallel evolution. Those beings couldn't have come from Earth."

"I know it," I admitted. "But just the same, they did. Not recently. Millennia ago. They're people-human. I'd swear it."

"You're tough and you're stubborn," Lindy said. "When

you get an idea, you really check it out. But you've got nothing to base this one on, old friend.''

"Then I'll find something," I vowed. "Somewhere, a basic premise is off-base. Let's hie home and get out of this blasted blue light. I've already forgotten what you really look like."

Chapter 3

When the *Stardust* showed in the distance, it was a welcome sight; infinitely more pleasing inside. There was light that was sensible; normal, blessed light. Split up by a prism, it would have made a spectrum. Lindy looked peaches and cream again. I suppose even I looked better. The best way to appreciate something is to be deprived of it, just like your Sunday-school teacher always told you. Try a stretch in a light where you can't see red or yellow or even violet. You'd miss 'em.

We showered and freshened up generally, then had a good meal. Rasmussen joined us. We reported while we ate, putting the talk on tape so we wouldn't have to go over it again. Johnny was in a silent, contemplative mood, but he squeezed the last detail out of us. His computer mind doesn't fit the rest of him.

"They seem very human, Roscoe," he said. "All the readings we could get are amazingly close to ours. Any ideas?"

"Just one," I said. "They *are* human."

Johnny warmed the tiny dash of brandy in his big snifter, his long, expressive fingers curled about it. "A very long chance, isn't it? They seem indigenous. What is your reasoning?"

"I don't have any," I admitted. "Every now and then I cut across lots. I'm intuitive. I have the gift of divination."

"You have the gift of conversation," Lindy said mildly. "You're covering, of course. He won't tell you, Johnny, until he gets his hunches and his facts sorted out. You know that."

Rasmussen sighed, and barely wet his lips with the brandy.

"I know," he said. "Only Dr. Williams does a better smoke screen."

"Speaking of whom," I said, "where is Pegleg? Shouldn't he be giving with the 'how I spent my day,' too?"

"He should, if he were back. He apparently found not only interesting geology, but intriguing artifacts as well. Mr. Price reports that he entered a canyon some forty kilometers from base, and that communication has become spotty and intermittent. But he assures us that he is in no difficulty. I have a manned scoutboat standing by."

"Every time he goes out, things get lively," I grumbled. "He's got everything but judgment."

"He has survived," Rasmussen said dryly.

"Yeah. One leg short. And that because he couldn't pass up a bet that he wouldn't swim across a little lagoon full of plesiosaurs."

"*Someone* offered the bet," the chief said.

"How could I know he'd try it? And after all, I *did* get him out."

"Roscoe," Lindy said indignantly, "you never told me that!"

"My dear," I said reasonably, "you never asked me."

We embroidered the edges of the report a little more; then Rasmussen left. Lindy and I talked idly for a bit. But we weren't relaxed. For me, that's unusual. I can take it easy anywhere. I suspected the blue light. There were no overt signs, but how could we really tell what exposure to it would do to us? Suppose we started to grow long and thin, like the blue slingmen?

We gave up, and went up to Main. About twenty people were there, mostly concerned with the appearance of twilight and night on this blue world.

Everyone knew what to expect. We had carefully recorded the planet's thirty-hour twenty-two-minute rotation. We had charted the orbits of its three moons; we had calculated their masses and distances from the planet; we were prepared for the fact that they would seem to swing across the night sky almost in line. We sat and watched it all—and once again just knowing wasn't enough. To see made it all different.

Most section chiefs and major researchers were in their own quarters or labs, using their own facilities for observation. The watchers here were mostly the more routine scientists, experts in techniques, but subject to direction. Don't misunderstand, though. They were all good, all highly selected. The *Stardust* carried no plain labor, and no drones.

Ursula Potts sat deep in an easy chair, the uncanny spectacle of the three moons on the screen before her. Actually, she's a small woman, and I almost missed her, sitting there in subdued light. Lindy and I have a special feeling for Ursula. She was with us when we made it official, that day after the strange battle on Cyrene IV, at the ceremony of honorable fusion of our colorful cubic friends of that most unusual planet.

"Plenty of room," Ursula said. She waved her skinny fingers at a nearby chair. It was the only one close to her not occupied.

"Be a mite snug, won't it? Count us. There's more than one."

"Married, aren't you? Like each other, don't you?" the old witch said. "Hold her on your lap."

At that, it wasn't a bad idea. The chair was sturdy and comfortable, and we were still on our honeymoon. Come to think of it, that honeymoon was approaching a record. It had been going on for ten years.

We watched the slow progress of the blue moons across the blue firmament. The brighter stars were cold blue points beyond. The chill seemed to creep from the screen. Gratefully, I hugged the warm girl on my lap.

"Ursula," I said, "why did you paint it blue, out yonder in orbit?"

Ursula pulled at her long nose. "Not sure, really. Felt blue. Felt cold, like that view. Had to be."

"We saw the blue men's village," I offered.

Ursula glanced briefly toward us.

"Heard," she said.

"I want you to paint it," I went on. "I see something there others don't see. I believe you'll see it, too."

"Soft soap," said Ursula.

I could feel Lindy giggle.

"It's not meant to be," I protested. "I'm in dead earnest, just like the two worms fighting. I need some support."

"Bad joke," Ursula's pale eyes had picked up the bleak blue of the screen. "Have to paint the village. You know that. Do it when you get me there. Won't take a jumper, though. Abominable things."

"Mighty handy at times, just the same. Especially in rough country."

"Don't go into rough country," Ursula said. "Bad enough being a pioneer in comfort."

I chuckled. I was pleased, too. Not many of the *Stardust*'s varied population ever saw this wryly humorous side of Ursula Potts. She was accorded a dubious respect, but she wasn't known.

"Bad joke," I said. "Contradiction in terms. But speaking of rough country, Pegleg is still out in all that blue chill." I slid my thumbnail into a communications crease in the chair arm. "Let's get the latest bulletin on him."

In a moment the chair mike gurgled softly.

"Price," it said.

"Roscoe, Stony," I said. "Something must be cooking or you'd be beddy-bye. What?"

"So would you. I suppose you're calling about Pegleg. He's okay. He's finally coming in."

"Any story?"

"Nothing I can make much sense of," Stony said. "But he's bubbling like a kettle. He crossed the line of foothills and went on into the mountains. Apparently he found deep canyons knifing into the range and followed one in. That's when we nearly lost his signal."

"I heard."

"About an hour ago, he came clear again. Sounded like he'd found a moonshine still in there somewhere. He was really chortling. He *said* he'd seen the Taj Mahal, Angkor Wat and the palace of Rameses II, all rolled together and improved on. Anyhow, he's riding the home beam like a stampeding kangaroo. He's really working that jumper."

"Good thing it's hard to wreck one," I said. "Thanks, Stony. You've set me mind easy."

I leaned back in the chair. Lindy squirmed on my lap and Ursula looked at me quizzically.

"Slings. Thatched shelters. A wheatfield fifteen miles square. The first two are not consistent with the last, but they're all believable."

"You're disappointed," Lindy said. "Our blue men are not the top culture of the planet after all. They're just primitives, living in the wilderness. The advanced race or races are in the mountains."

"The slingmen are *men*," I insisted. "Earth was their mother. And where men are, men rule."

"Your species conceit is aching," my wife said. "Logically, that doesn't have to be, as well you know. And the probability that the blue men are of Earth origin also approaches zero."

"A contentious woman is more obnoxious than a fly in the soup," I said. "An intelligent woman carefully hides the fact. And the greatest tragedy of all would be if you should happen to be right."

Ursula stood up. "Leaping at conclusions," she observed. "Not like you. Get more data! I'm going to bed."

"You see," I said to Lindy. "Not an unwise word in the whole batch."

"I know. *She's* a woman," Lindy pointed out, and thus had the last word.

Chapter 4

We hadn't waited up for Pegleg. When we heard that he was in no trouble, we seemed suddenly to relax. Adjustment to a new life situation always takes it out of me, and when I reach a certain point, I sack out and sleep around the clock. Then I'm ready to go.

So I heard Pegleg's story only after it was common knowledge all over the ship. Still, that didn't hurt it any. It was quite a yarn. I heard it with my midday breakfast, for when I didn't show up at the morning conference, Pegleg came to me. He knew my habits.

He gave me the gist, half stretched out in an easy chair and slurping a cup of my coffee.

"Roscoe, we've seen ruins, you and I. We've seen deserted cities and all kinds of barbaric remnants and artifacts. And you can believe me—we never saw anything like this."

"Deserted?" That bothered me. "You're sure?"

"The only route in was a trail through the canyon. A worn track, like a game trail. The amphitheater is maybe a couple of miles across and four or five long, a big elliptical bowl. The walls go up a thousand, two thousand feet in some places."

"And full of buildings."

"*Not* full of buildings. They were around the cliff bases. The floor of the bowl is like a park. It's landscaped, with paths through it in stylized patterns. The vegetation is spaced. Looks like they just left it yesterday."

"Maybe they did," I said. "And maybe they'll be back tomorrow."

Pegleg shook his head. His narrow face showed a baffled earnestness.

"I counted one hundred thirty-three structures, ranging from small, simple houses with one entrance to the great cathedral at the end of the amphitheater."

"Cathedral?"

"That's what it looked like. It must be a block or more across the front, and the highest spires go up five, six hundred feet. It might have held thousands of people—but for one thing."

"Which is?"

"Roscoe, none of those buildings was built. They were carved! They're around the cliff bases because they are a part of the cliffs. They are chiseled right out of the walls themselves. Fine, textured granite, hard and beautiful for carving, and just about indestructible."

I had finished my eggs and toast. I poured another cup of coffee and passed the pot over to Pegleg.

"Pegleg," I said, "yesterday I got an impression that the blue light was affecting me. I was jumpy, edgy. How about you? You're sure you saw all this?"

Pegleg grinned. "I saw it," he said. "I'll take you there. In fact, Bud Merani is all set up, with a twenty-man team ready to go. He'd be on his way but for the organization meeting tomorrow."

Bud Merani is chief archaeologist. Like every researcher aboard, his enthusiasm drives him. He loves remnants of cultures and technologies like Don Juan loved blondes and brunettes, like Cap'n Jules loves his engines. Without that special delight in his field, Johnny Rasmussen wouldn't give any man ship-room.

Pegleg and I talked it out, just as we had hundreds of times before. We made plans. The contented feeling that gradually takes over when there's a new job to do had claimed us both.

"Meanwhile," I said, "back at the ranch, or rather the wheatfield. . . . You've been briefed on the slingmen? Didn't see any, I take it."

"Nary a one," Pegleg said. "I think they're nothing but figments."

"Go out without a forcefield up," I suggested. "Wander around the grainfield. They'll bounce a figment off you that will be remarkably like a rock. Talk about catapults! That's what they are. Human catapults, with guidance systems yet."

Pegleg shifted in his chair, eased his knee and looked quizzical.

"Human?"

I nailed him with a mean stare.

"You too, huh?" I said. "My fame, my prestige, my acknowledged preeminence as an ecologist—these mean nothing to you? Perhaps you might be interested in a small wager?"

Pegleg patted his plastic knee. "Wagers with you," he said, "have been known to result in some personal inconvenience."

"Low blow," I said. "We were younger and more foolish then."

"Younger, anyway," Pegleg grinned. "Roscoe, I'm a rock man. A lot of the people we know back on Earth don't seem very human to me. So if you say the blue boys are Earth spawn I'll go along, even if it ain't a popular position. In fact, *because* it ain't."

"Back in the twentieth century," I said, "you would have grown a straggly beard and marched in protest parades."

The planning meeting came as scheduled. We all stated our impressions of things in general, and indicated our proposed courses of action. As usual, they were approved. Rasmussen agrees that we know more about our respective fields than anybody else possibly could. What he insists on are clear understandings on location, logistics, and safety. When we get lost, as we do, he likes to know where to look.

One by one the scoutboats hissed softly out of their slips, carrying the mapping boys, the wind and cloud chasers, the zoological survey teams, the plant pressers. Ursula Potts had her little transparent studio extruded and sat in comfort high above the waving wheat, painting the blue land. Merani's archaeologists left by jumper.

Lindy, Pegleg, and I lingered. We've worked together so much that a great deal of what we do seems almost instinctive. We dawdled now. I'm not sure I know why, but we all reacted the same way. We just weren't ready to go yet.

"Over there!" Lindy pointed. "Beyond that knoll. What is it?"

I picked it up and put a glass on it. It was moving along at a crawl, but steadily, heading purposefully for the *Stardust*.

"Model T," Pegleg said.

The thing had four enormous wheels, very thin, but projecting high above the grain, higher even than the blue slingmen who glided along beside it.

We watched. It didn't hesitate. If the blue men hadn't before realized the significance of the *Stardust*, they did now. They came on with a courage you had to appreciate.

"What makes it go?"

That wasn't hard to see. Suspended high between the wheels was a flat wagon body, and on it a single blue man bowed and straightened as he worked a long lever.

"Manpower," Pegleg said in astonishment. "A simple belt drive."

The thing rolled toward us. As we watched, another man boarded it, took over the lever, and the other dropped to the ground.

"They change off," I said. "Probably hard work."

"Erudite," said Pegleg.

We were outside, sprawled on a jumper platform even higher than Ursula's studio. We could easily be seen.

"I feel a little naked out here," I said. "They could pick us off like Robin Hood if the spirit moved them."

"Rocks bounce off us," Lindy reminded. "Remember?"

The cart rolled to a stop below us. Ten slingmen stood motionless, looking up. Then one stepped forward and extended a long arm.

"F'iend!" His high voice carried.

"It's our old buddy," I said. "I recognize him by the wart on his chin."

My wife looked at me pityingly.

"That would be the way," she said.

The tall, thin figures stood at silent, courteous attention. They waited patiently. It was our move.

"Well, go on," Lindy said. Like all women, she fidgets. "You big chief. Make with the palaver!"

I leaned over the edge of the platform, extended my own

arm, and said "Friend!" in a good loud voice. Then I added, "Just a sec! We'll be right down!"

"*That* should hold 'em!" Pegleg said.

We entered the platform port, dropped by small lift to ground level, and slid out an exit platform into the grain. We were outside again in less than a minute.

I began to suspect that the long blue faces of the slingmen were incapable of showing expression. They stood as we had left them. Our miraculous disappearance and reappearance apparently left them unmoved. They simply looked at us with unwinking attention.

"Nice rig you have there," I remarked in a conversational tone. I waved a hand at it.

The tall leader stepped forward a pace. It *was* the same fellow who had used me for a target. He was taller, wider, a little more of everything than the others. He didn't offer to shake hands.

But he raised a hand, said "F'iend" again, then gestured toward the cart. The motive power up there promptly handed down what looked like a long roll of paper. With great dignity the blue leader extended it to me. He still showed no emotion, but I could sense an excitement in him. His blue slanted slits of eyes seemed to gleam in his blue face.

"Well, thank you!" I said.

I held it up, turned it end to end. It was more like plastic than paper.

"Pegleg, let's unroll this. I think we're expected to."

It unrolled readily, although it had held its tight roll without a fastener. And even in the blue light we knew we had something really different, really puzzling.

"Blimey!" Pegleg said. He spoke with deep feeling as he stared. I heard Lindy catch her breath, and I don't think I made any sound at all.

It looked like a photograph, which was unlikely enough considering the cultural level of the slingmen. But it was too stylized, too perfect. A quick look with a lens showed me the fine lines of an amazingly intricate drawing. Doubtless it was in color, but only good light would show that.

The picture was remarkable enough, a vast building with arches, long, graceful windows, and sky-reaching spires.

But along its base, dwarfed by it, but perfectly depicted, were people. Not long and blue people—people like us, wearing strange, elaborate costumes.

The eagerness of the blue men showed through their expressionless calm.

"Lovely!" Lindy said.

"Remarkable," I said. "Any ideas, Pegleg?"

Pegleg's narrow face showed both puzzlement and glee. "Roscoe, the longer I live the more convinced I am that there's no such thing as coincidence. But I've seen that building—that's the cathedral!"

I studied the skeletal slingmen, then looked back at the recognizable human figures of the drawing. In spite of everything, I was conscious of a vague disappointment. The pattern was apparent. A civilization had waxed, waned, and disappeared; and its artifacts were treasured by surviving primitives. But then I realized that the problem hadn't changed. Where had the people come from? Where were they now?

The tall leader of the blue men suddenly took over. He stepped forward, and aimed a long finger at me, tapped his own bony rib cage, and pointed to the picture. Then he faced about and swept his arm toward the distant mountains. I didn't react. After a minute, he went through the whole routine again.

"I follow you, pal," I said. "*You* will guide *me* into the *mountains* and show me that *building.*"

I repeated his motions and nodded my head. With Pegleg's help I rolled the picture and offered it back to him. But he wouldn't take it. He pointed to it, then to me, then held both palms out.

"It's yours, Roscoe," Pegleg said. "Courtesy of the Establishment."

Lindy took it from my hand. She held it cradled in her arms, smiled and bowed slightly. The blue man studied her, then bowed in return.

"It'll be lovely in our bedroom," Lindy said. "I know just where I'm going to hang it."

"And so much for the archaeological find of the planet thus far!" Pegleg's disgust was not entirely feigned. He loves them, but women don't make an awful lot of sense to him. They don't to me either, but I've adjusted to it. He never will.

He strolled over to examine the blue men's high-wheeled vehicle. They watched him with cold, unmoving detachment. The design of the thing obviously had a purpose, and after a few minutes I thought I saw what it was. The wagon bed sat high above the wheel axles, braced firmly in place on strutlike projections. The entire assembly was higher than the tops of the grain stalks. The narrow wheels caused little grain damage. The cart had left almost no trail across the field.

"Grain cart?" I suggested. "Probably a harvest cart. They used it today because they wanted to make an impression."

"Ten men, if men they be, and this contraption, just to deliver one picture?" Pegleg was dubious. "Maybe they jest dooes things de hahd way."

"Formality. Dignity. This whole bit is a big deal for them, and I'm not at all sure we know what they're trying to get across. The picture doesn't seem something they'd be likely to give away. I wonder," I mused, "if it has occurred to them how like we are to the people shown there. Maybe they gave it to us because they think it's ours."

"Speaking of which," Lindy said, "what can we give in return? Exchange of presents is a very *human* custom." She winked at me.

"Pictures," Pegleg suggested promptly. "I've got a stack of *Stardust* prints on my desk. Those ought to slant their eyes."

"Good," I said. "Would you get 'em? One for each man, but a bigger one for the chief."

Lindy snapped slender fingers. "And Old Reliables, of course! I'll get some."

They both disappeared into the port. The slingmen watched with inscrutable intentness. They had to be mystified, or at least curious, but you'd never have known it. I just stood. In a few minutes Pegleg and Lindy were back.

Pegleg went from man to man, handing each a crisp 8 × 10 photograph of the *Stardust,* lying at length on a sunny hillside on some planet light-years away. In the blue light the color was lost. The leader got a 10 × 16, and his had men standing outside. The slingmen handled the prints gingerly.

Their immobile faces were as close to expression as we had yet seen them come.

But it was Lindy who broke through. She brought Old Reliables, a big handful. We had offered them on twenty planets, and they never failed. Lollipops! Each man got one on a stick of handy length. I suppose the flavors varied. Again the leader got the largest, a big, striped wafer that in normal light would have been red and white. I suspect our chances of continued cooperation from the slingmen depended for a moment on whether or not the big fellow would like peppermint.

As it chanced, he did. Lindy showed them what to do, holding a stick and putting the candy into her own mouth. Pegleg and I each demonstrated, exaggerating the gusto. The chief extended his blue tongue, gingerly, and in a couple of minutes every man was happily polishing a lollipop.

It was a pleasant little interlude. To see those gaunt gangling blue skeletons eating lollipops like nursery schoolers was something that couldn't even be imagined in another context. But with us the improbable was the usual, and the impossible happened all the time.

Lindy is a galactic microbiologist, perhaps the very best, but when she's out with me she doesn't work at it. Actually, she has a sociological knack. She can get through to the most unlikely life-forms. She's everything's friend.

And right there in front of the *Stardust,* while we all savored our lollipops, she taught the blue men to smile. Or rather, she taught the leader. Then, when he gave the word, *everybody* smiled. I kid you not—that's the way it worked.

She stood in front of the strange blue chief, her head thrown back, looking up at him as though he were Mount McKinley. She'd taste her candy, register satisfaction, and smile. Then she'd point at him, make finger motions of spreading her mouth. He caught on fast. He was no dummy. In fact, he was sharp. For he not only grasped the mechanics of the smile; he savvied its meaning. And of course he'd seen us grinning at each other. More and more I got the impression that the cold scrutiny that the blue men gave everything was just as intent as it looked. They didn't miss much.

And when the chief finally smiled, you should have seen what it did to his face. I wouldn't have believed it. As the slitlike mouth widened, even, perfect rows of blue teeth showed. The cold slant eyes crinkled. The long face softened. For a fleeting moment, that impressive beanpole of a man looked genuinely pleasant.

"At-a-boy!" Lindy gurgled. "I knew you could do it!"

Her smile widened into a happy laugh. She actually danced before him, looking up at him, her glee and pleasure most apparent. And, as I said, he caught on. His own smile widened. When her laugh became audible, deep sounds came out of his bony chest, sounds quite unlike the high tones he used in speaking. The barrier broke. They stood laughing at each other, the lovely Earth female and the towering blue slingman of the planet Hadorn.

I found myself grinning. Pegleg couldn't help it either, though he was a little sour about it. The blue leader, still smiling, turned to his silent companions. He spoke two high, crisp words. And they smiled. By the numbers. But I sensed that they were real smiles. They, too, had grasped the meaning of this curious custom of we strange people.

To make friends, you act friendly. You have friendly gestures, friendly symbols in common. Lindy's lesson in smiling was the major breakthrough. It was only a step, then, to name calling.

My wife pointed to herself, said "Lindy!"; to me, "Roscoe!"; to Pegleg, said "Pegleg!" Then she pointed to the tall chief, raised her eyebrows, tried to get the question across. He smiled tentatively. She went through it again. You could see him get it. Once she had relaxed his face to smile, it began to show varied expressions.

He pointed to her. "Lindy!" he said carefully. He switched cold eyes to me: "Osco!" At Pegleg he said "Peleg!" He couldn't handle that first G. But then he turned his long finger toward himself and said triumphantly, "San!"

Again he and Lindy laughed. I don't know how she does it. I know only that I'm proud.

We all said "San!" He gave us each his versions of our names. I looked at the other blue men, but he didn't offer to introduce them. I didn't push it. There was no knowing their social organization, and I wasn't about to trample any taboos. Time would work it out.

Then, abruptly, the blue men terminated the parley. I'd been cogitating on inviting them in, but apparently they had had all they could take. The chief gave no orders. They simply spun their cart around, the boy at the lever began to work, and away they went. If they knew good-bye, they didn't waste it on us. When they were fifty yards away, though, tall San turned and briefly raised a long arm. We waved in answer. After that no one looked back.

We watched them dwindle.

Lindy held the rolled picture in her arms. She patted it, looking thoughtful.

I turned my gaze on Pegleg. "Figments!" I said.

Chapter 5

Then we got busy. The picture had changed things. We had Stony Price catch the archaeologists and brief them. Although the amphitheater had looked deserted, Pegleg admitted that it probably wasn't so. The trail showed little travel, but that didn't signify. There were doubtless other ways to get in.

The blue men knew all about the buildings; that was evident. San had offered to show me, but then had left before I could take him up on it. But he had given me the picture. That was important, but for the life of me I couldn't figure out why.

We studied it carefully back in my lab—Pegleg and Lindy and I, and special invited guest Dr. Johannes Rasmussen. Under perfect light it was a spectacular work of art, and, as I had suspected, wrought in delicate and varied colors. It consisted entirely of fine pen lines, and the work must have been done under magnification, or else by beings that had vision far superior to ours. The colored inks ran the gamut of shadings. The painstaking precision of every line, the crisp perfection of the finished work, indicated patience, much time, and superior craftsmanship as well as art.

"This isn't the cathedral I saw," Pegleg said. "This is the original. This is a picture of the model from which that was carved."

"Brought here from somewhere else?" I suggested. "From a planet with color, a planet with a yellow sun? Like Earth, perhaps?"

Pegleg grinned across the table. "Why not?" he said. He loves the long chance, the unlikely solution. He's an ornery genius.

"Certainly somewhere else," Rasmussen agreed.

39

"Somewhere with color. But not Earth. You know that, Roscoe. And Dr. Williams is just being cantankerous because that's how he gets his kicks. He doesn't believe it."

Pegleg's narrow face was grave, but his glee showed in his eyes. "Such language from a director! Man hears something new every day. Why shouldn't I believe it? Roscoe's a cagy thinker on these evolution and adaptation bits. Probably number one, when you come to that. Why shouldn't I go along?"

Rasmussen's voice took on the tone and timbre of the college professor he once had been. "The first men from Earth invaded space in A.D. 1968, a simple little slingshot flight out and around the Moon. Just one hundred fifty-two years ago. We've been out of the Solar System fifteen years —just since Ultraspan." He paused and looked at us impressively. "These are facts. Every schoolboy knows them."

"Every schoolgirl too, Johnny," Lindy cut in. "We admit your facts. That's what makes it tricky. Those are *people* on that drawing. *Earth* people!"

She'll argue with me in private, but out among our peers we're a solid team.

Rasmussen molded the needle points of his moustache with long fingers. He rarely debated. He retired from the lectern now. "Perhaps," he admitted, "though I've never seen an Earth drawing like this."

"Nor I," I agreed.

"The material on which the drawing is made is unfamiliar, isn't it?"

"Completely," I said. "Chem lab's analyzing that corner I snipped off down there. I hated to mutilate it, but it seemed necessary."

Rasmussen turned to Pegleg. "It took time to carve this structure in granite—wouldn't you say so, Dr. Williams?"

"Hundreds, maybe thousands of years," Pegleg granted readily. "And that's with no labor problems and no strikes."

"But Earthmen did it? People of Earth origin?"

"Roscoe says so. I'll go along."

"And you can't support your contentions, Dr. Kissinger?"

"Not reasonably," I said. "I have a hypothesis, though. It

doesn't grab anybody but me, so I'll keep it classified until we look about some more. Because don't forget my corollary. The blue men are human, too.''

Rasmussen smiled. I could see that he was completely content. Everybody was challenged; everything was functioning. We were on the ball. We'd work out the problems. We always had.

Chapter 6

Bud Merani was a small, slender, swarthy man, with the full lips and glowing dark eyes of his East Indian heritage. With his tiny feet and woman's delicate hands he always gave a hothouse impression, an effete, purposeless sort of look. I don't know a tougher field man.

After Rasmussen left, we sat in my lab and listened to tapes of Merani's contacts with Stony Price. The tapes are a part of a recorder bank, and you can punch for anything you want, played back on your own duplicator.

The archaeologists had reached the amphitheater. Communication was rocky, as it had been with Pegleg. But there were fragments.

"Incredible place!" one segment reported. "We have not yet deployed into small study groups. The evidences of recent occupation are too plain. These bas reliefs are more than that. I am convinced that space lies behind them."

Pegleg nodded. "That's the way I felt. The light was already failing when I got there, though, and those deep blue shadows were nasty. Most of what I saw was by magnaflash."

A later bit reported: "We're setting up camp in the park in front of the cathedral. 'Park' is correct. There are paths laid out. The vegetation is thinned and pruned. The whole scene is current.

"We're staying together in jumper teams, so as to be near the forcefields. Should have brought forcefield belts. We're being watched. Bound to be."

A third fragment said: "Sun below the cliffs now. Shadows deepening. Temps not bad, but this blue light is as bleak as an Arctic scene. We're building fires. They make a big difference."

I shut off the duplicator. "We've frittered away the day," I said. "Out there in the blue twilight people are rushing about, being overt, learning things. How have we justified our presence here? Why shouldn't we be sent home?"

Lindy leaned back luxuriously in my best padded chair. "We haven't even earned a before-dinner pick-me-up," she agreed happily. "Let's have one anyhow."

"I think I'll just have bourbon," Pegleg said. "No ice."

The following day we became overt ourselves. I was beginning to itch to get at some representative ecosystem studies, but, as usual, the dominant species problems had to be resolved first. And here, on this planet of all blue light, they promised to be major. So at blue sunrise we headed for the village.

This time we used the jeep. Oh, I know. Mostly they exist in museums and hobbyists' collections, back on that small, sunny and still green planet that is home. But this one had been adapted. It still looked like a World War II model, except for the tracks. It was Pegleg's pride. When its like had first been designed, nobody could have imagined the unknown worlds on which it finally would be driven.

Pegleg had wheels, and he used them when the country was open. But today we would have to fight the wheat. Though there would be damage, we decided that it was justified. The jumpers were handy, but the jeep was practically self-contained. Its motive force, a timonium power pill, will go on practically forever, although Pegleg replaces it every half-million miles. Its forcefield is a rugged unit. It can resist raw energies that would destroy the jumpers.

At twenty-five miles an hour, you have time to think and look and appreciate. And that's as fast as the tracks would go. We plowed along on the jumper route Lindy and I had followed, then skirted the edge of the grainfield. I had figured the village at fifteen miles from the ship, and even with the dog-leg we made, I was pretty close.

"Look for the neon signs," I advised Pegleg. "There's one over every nightclub."

"Turn left at the blue Sally Rand poster," Lindy directed. "It'll take you right onto Main Street."

Our driver looked at us pityingly. He punched the force-field button and the tiny indicator light came on. It was red, so in this light you could hardly see it.

"Just in case the police don't have the demonstrators under complete control," he said loftily. "We aren't blue, you know. And probably only blue is really beautiful."

Off to our right was the rockpile from which Lindy and I had made our observations. Ahead was the bleak blue ripple and flow of the river.

"If we're lucky," I said, "San is the police chief. Also the mayor, the chief municipal judge, and the official greeter. At least we can say we're visiting him."

"Really?" Pegleg sounded like an old lady at a tea-party. "What are you going to use for words?"

"My sign talk is known even out where the stars are thin," I said. "And we do have the man's name."

Pegleg eased the jeep down the slope toward the river. And from the docks and narrow boats along the beach, blue slingmen sprouted like the children of the dragon's teeth.

How those cadaverous Slim Jims could move! They whispered through the grain like eels, weaving as they ran. It was, I recognized, a practiced thing. Even with a rifle or a ray they would have been hard to hit. With a sling I'd have said it would have been close to impossible. Unless, that is, you were another slingman.

"I only hope San isn't the leader of the loyal opposition," said Pegleg dryly. "Could be he isn't even from this settlement. We're so confident we're losing our smarts. We could have reconned this whole area from a scoutboat."

"Let's go back and do it," I suggested.

We grinned at each other and at the tightening ring of blue men, each with a sling at ready and a stone in place. We were secure behind our forcefield, and knew it. As it turned out, they knew it, too. Apparently our wide smiles were the key.

Two slingmen darted forward from the ring. They furled their slings around their right forearms and returned rocks to bags with that fluid sleight-of-hand motion. They stood, gaunt and erect in the path of the jeep, and held up right hands. "F'iend!" they said as one man. Then, mechanically but genuinely, they smiled.

We were down to five miles an hour anyway, so Pegleg brought us to a stop.

"Cut the forcefield, Pegleg," I said. "We know these boys. They have eaten our lollipops."

Pegleg raised his eyebrows, but he punched the button. I climbed out.

The long blue faces of twenty skeleton men did not change as I walked confidently up to the smiling two. I reached out, shook each hand in turn.

"Friend!" I said. And smiled.

They smiled wider, and echoed my sentiments. Then, their faces still again, they turned and beckoned and started to walk toward the river.

We were parked on a level spot just beyond the edge of the grain. The riverbank was hard and beaten. The endless tramp of bare feet had reduced it almost to a cementlike state. And at its edge were the log and stone docks, with a dozen slender needlelike boats moored alongside.

I started to follow, then stopped. "I don't rightly know about this," I said. "You two better stay with the forcefield. One's enough to exchange courtesies."

Lindy unloaded her graceful self promptly.

"I didn't come to stay in the jeep," she said pleasantly. "I haven't visited anybody in ever so long. Further, *I* taught them to smile. They'll definitely expect *me!*"

Pegleg did things to the controls of the jeep, set them on remote, and put the switch in his pocket. With that handy gadget, he can call the jeep to him from up to a mile away.

"Never shall it be said," he remarked, "that Williams deserted friends in peril. Especially," he added, "since I doubt that there's any danger anyway."

I expected nothing else, but I had to give them their chances to be independent. It's a pattern we observe.

I gestured to the waiting slingmen. "Lead on, Macduff!" I said. "Alert the ferry! We can ride anything you can!"

"I'm sort of glad they can't understand you," Lindy said. She held my arm in a phony show of delicacy. "They'd be sure to get the wrong impression."

A slingman slipped into the stern of each of three splinter boats. These were, on closer inspection, beautifully crafted,

shell-like dugouts. I suspected that they could really skim the
water, and I knew they'd be tippy. We were each waved to a
different boat. Then the bow of each was manned by another
slingman. Lindy and I had got the two smilers, leaving
Pegleg alone with total strangers. He didn't seem to mind.

Our paddlers pushed off. The boats slipped soundlessly
over the cold blue water. There was only a slight current, and
the blue men ignored it. Behind us, boat after boat left the
docks. The small flotilla darted around us. Every dugout
bristled with gaunt blue slingmen, their death's-head faces as
bleak as the blue river. Yet I knew they were coming along
out of curiosity. They just didn't want to miss anything.

"My paddlers can beat your paddlers!" Lindy called from
amidships her slender craft. The middle seats were comfortable. There were even handholds on either side.

"I don't know how to say 'giddap,'" I said. "Anyhow,
no racing room. We've arrived."

And so we had. Each stern paddler brought his boat alongside a pier as neatly as ever a sagamore handled his birchbark.
Both men were out of my craft and were steadying it for me to
step ashore.

"Slick, quick, and neat," Pegleg said. "The news has
gotten about."

We were not rushed or crowded. No disorderly rabble
streamed down to the river. People were in evidence, though.
At closer vantage the conical thatch-covered shelters seemed
a bit larger and more sturdy than they had at a distance.
There was a family group by each. They stared at us with
slanted, cold, unwinking blue eyes. We stared back just as
frankly.

Poor Pegleg! The women looked almost exactly like the
men. They were slighter, smaller, with no more hair on their
long heads, and no more clothing. The fact that they were
mammals was plain for all to see, but none of them could
have cracked the Folies-Bergère. They wore breech coverings, no ornaments, and each had a knife precisely like the
men.

No man had eyebrows, but every woman had them, broad
emphatic arches of royal blue. Painted on, of course. When I
thought about it, why "of course"? It was the only attempt at

ornamentation we had seen. And why eyebrows? Since nobody had them, where had the idea come from?

Lindy was thinking along the same lines.

"If I were any good at it," she said, "I could set up a beauty shop here. I'd make a fortune."

We had paused to look around. Our guides stood waiting for us, immobile, inscrutable.

"Maybe they like themselves the way they are," I suggested. "And if the matter of legal tender came up, as it would, what would you accept for pay?"

"A point," my wife admitted. "I'll ponder it."

We strolled slowly through the bleak community, following hard-beaten paths that wandered almost at random between the irregularly spaced shelters. The great metallic columns of tree trunks lifted with the same lack of arrangement, almost without branches for a hundred feet up, then breaking into clusters of blue foliage that filtered and reduced the light of the blue sun.

"There!" Peg pointed. "We're in the right town after all."

One of our *Stardust* photos was conspicuously displayed on a shelter, stuck in a crevice in the rough wall beside the entrance. A tall blue slingman stood beside it, with his slender blue woman and two much smaller editions of themselves. We approached, the man stepped forward, held out his hand and smiled.

"F'iend!" he said.

I responded in kind, then Pegleg, then Lindy.

"We must teach them something else," Lindy said. "A one-word vocabulary is definitely limiting."

"Why not teach him?" Pegleg suggested. "He looks as smart as any of them."

"The things you can see!" Lindy said admiringly. "He looks just like all the others to me. But I think not. The lady and I have more in common."

She held out slender fingers to the blue woman.

"Friend," she said, and smiled her nicest, which, you may remember, is very nice indeed.

The blue girl glanced briefly at her tall consort, then looked steadily at Lindy. Slowly she extended a surprisingly grace-

ful hand. She struggled with facial muscles that had been
immobile all her life. She raised her painted blue brows. Her
thin mouth twisted, but a smile formed. Then you might say
that it broke through, as though it had been there all the time
and nobody knew it. Her teeth showed, and her voice came
out with a high lilt.

"F'iend!" Her delight was evident, and she and my hyp-
notic wife beamed at each other, and the handshake was
fervent and prolonged.

Lindy followed up promptly. She pointed to herself and
said "woman." Then to the blue girl and repeated
"woman." She pointed to the slingman, said "man," and
then to Pegleg and to me, each time speaking the word. The
blue girl's intent face was far more expressive than even
San's had been. You could see her catch on.

She pointed to her husband and said "man." Her face was
almost impish as she pronounced the word. Her blue finger
turned to me. I, it seemed, also was "man." As was Pegleg.
Then she indicated herself and said "wo-man" very precisely. And Lindy was also "wo-man." Her face, more
expressive every minute, fairly lighted in the blue gloom.

"F'iend!" She almost squealed, and held out both hands
to Lindy, exactly as women on Earth have been doing for
many thousands of years.

The grim slingman was watching with the cold, expressionless concentration they seemed to give to everything.
And I watched him. He did not smile, but his death's-head
face underwent a subtle transformation, for all that. I think I
felt rather than saw it. He was looking at the blue girl the way
I look at Lindy. It was a fond, indulgent look. He was proud
of his woman!

Sure, I knew it had to be, but it took some getting used to.
You have to know people to find out what they're like. And I
had ample evidence that these had a high order of intelligence. I couldn't equate that with the crude shelters, the lack
of clothing and ornaments, the primitive weapons. But I
knew it was so.

Pegleg was never as sensitive and as concerned with living
creatures as Lindy and I. Maybe it's his preoccupation with
rocks. More likely, it's just the way he is. He's still my best

friend, the man I can depend on when the chips are really down. So it didn't bother me when he said, "Very touching and all that, but this could take all day, Roscoe. Learning a language takes time. We may be lousing up protocol fraternizing with the citizens instead of going straight to San."

"San!" The blue slingman picked that up instantly. And our two guides, who had been standing impassively, forgotten and left out, also stepped forward. "San!" one of them said. He motioned and turned.

"Go pay our respects," Lindy said. "I think I'll stay here and visit." She saw my dubious look and added, "I'll be safe. If I weren't, I'd have the feeling. And San won't expect consistency from a woman. My friend here and I are more alike than you think."

"I see the resemblances," I admitted. "But if you don't mind, I do applaud the differences, too. Have fun. I know you'll be safe."

In spite of what I've just said about him, sometimes Pegleg will fool you. He did now. The two small offspring of our blue host and hostess had been standing, like our guides, unnoticed. Pegleg bent, offered a forefinger to each, smiled and said "Friend!"

Like your children and the ones I hope to have, they didn't respond. They didn't do anything, just stared at him out of expressionless, slanted blue eyes. After a moment Pegleg chuckled, patted each on the top of his long, fuzzy-topped head, and turned away. But I knew he had gained face with their impassive parents. You can bet he knew it, too.

We followed our guides, now three, for the family man had joined the others. Doubtless they, as members of the squad that had visited the *Stardust,* all felt a proprietary responsibility for us. We didn't let them drag us along fast though, even if, as we assumed, the chief's house was our destination. We strolled, stopped and looked, commented.

"Roscoe," Pegleg said, "did you notice those kids?"

"I saw," I admitted.

"By stretching it a little, they could almost have been your kids or mine."

"I hope to do better," I said, "but they do look a lot more like standard-type humans than their parents."

"They had hair," Pegleg said. "The adults don't. They have vestiges of eyebrows. Adults, none, except for the ladies' blue paint. Those two weren't elongated. They were almost plump."

"Young often show ancestral traits." I indicated another juvenile by a shelter we were passing. He was older, longer, more skeletal.

"Teen-ager," Pegleg said. "As they grow, they change. I want to see an infant."

"Giving up geology?" I asked. "You're getting along to change emphasis like that."

Pegleg grinned. "Man should be broad," he said.

"Then you should be starting," I said. "Never too late, you know. Let's go see San!"

Our guides appreciated our sudden decision to hurry, I think. The settlement was not large, but the scattered, random distribution of the shelters made it seem so. It was impossible to travel in a straight line. I counted houses, but they looked so much alike, plus the fact that we seemed partially to be traveling in circles, that I soon knew my count was pointless. There had to be several hundred shelters, though.

We weren't taken to a home. Instead we circled into a little clearing, open to the blue light and almost cheerful from the pulsing redness of a number of small fires. The fires were a surprise, though I knew that in reason they would be familiar with them. In the high oxygen atmosphere they glowed hotly, but the redness showed only when we were close enough to feel the heat.

They were cookfires. Over some of them kettles bubbled. Over others, meat roasted. Blue men and blue women, perhaps a score or more, worked with the food. It looked like the beginning of a celebration or a feast. But no gaiety. The people looked at us, but they didn't stop their work or greet us. Their emotionless, expressionless faces, cold and still, told us nothing. But San was there. He strode toward us.

"F'iend!"

He held out his long blue hand, shook hands with each of us, smiled.

"Osco!"

"Pe-leg!"

We smiled and said "San!"

He looked about.

"Lindy?" You could hear the question in it, though he didn't raise his voice as we do.

I gestured in the general direction of where I thought we'd left her.

"She sent her regrets," I explained. "She's visiting with a friend."

He smiled, then directed a sharp, high-pitched sentence to our guides. One answered. It seemed to satisfy him.

The cooking layout was pretty extensive. I felt sure San had been notified as soon as we showed by the river. Still, the makings of a fiesta had been put together with admirable speed. Or so we thought.

As it turned out, the arrangements were not for us. When we had a chance to look around, the permanent nature of the place was apparent. The number of blue people in the glade didn't increase, but they came and went continually. Several rude slab tables held stacks of metallic-looking bowls, trencherlike dishes, piles of small round ladles with handles, two-tined forks.

Several men tended the fires. A couple or so kept check on the roasting meat and gave the kettles an occasional stir with flat paddles. But most of the blue people were simply serving themselves and departing with a trencher, a tray, or even several bowls of food. And, lest I neglect to mention it, a nice savory odor drifted about. It was mostly from the meat. There didn't seem to be much variety, but there was plenty. The why of that, too, was soon apparent.

A couple of the blue women set a metallic pot on one of the nearby slab tables. One of them poured grain from a jar into it. The other added water from another jar. Then they shredded into the mixture a handful of dried blue leaves. The pot was hung on the support over an unoccupied fire. Then each took a bowl and ladle, filled from an already steaming pot, and left the glade.

San stood by while we looked. He smiled politely. And after a few minutes he gestured toward the table with the utensils.

"We're being invited to dinner," Pegleg said. Then he added, "I think."

Actually, there was no doubt of it. The tall slingman strode to the nearest spit of roasting meat, drew his knife, and prepared to carve. There was no way to tell what the meat was. In a situation like this, faith helps a lot. I also hoped he had washed his knife since the last time I'd seen him use it. Then he had been flicking the heads off the grainfield "birds."

I held out a trencher and accepted a smoking-hot slab. San carved for Pegleg, then served himself. We each took a bowl and San ladled them full. Meat and vegetables. That seemed to be it. The big fellow beckoned, and we followed his gaunt muscular back.

I had seen the narrow slab tables here and there along the twisty trail through the settlement. We stopped at the first one we came to, pulled up the bench, set down our dishes—and dinner was served.

"Simple and handy," Pegleg said. "I wonder what they do when it rains."

That, I recalled, was something we hadn't yet seen. But the vegetation grew; the ground in shadow was moist; the air was reasonably humid. The blue clouds were scattered and fleecy, like any clear, mild summer day on Earth. There would be rain.

We each wore a knife. We drew them and imitated our host in cutting up our meat. San would cut a long, slender strip, pick it up by one end, put the other end into his slitlike mouth and solemnly chew until he reached the holding fingers. Then he'd take a ladle of the vegetable-grain mix and pour it in. He did it so neatly. It was fascinating to watch.

We tried not to imagine what we might be eating. We cut strips of the meat and chewed away. It wasn't bad. Add a little hunger, and we soon cleaned up our portions, becoming more skillful with each strip of meat. The dimensions of the furniture handicapped us somewhat, for they were structured for the blue people, of course, and even the ladies were seven feet tall. You feel silly sitting on a bench so high your feet don't touch the ground.

Gestures and sign language are all very well, but I always

try to dispense with them as soon as possible. I began the process while we ate. With primitives I try to teach them our language rather than learn theirs, mainly because I can take the initiative. My objective is communication, not language study. We leave that to the etymologists. Further, good old English is much more versatile than any speech they are likely to have.

By the meal's end we had got "food" and "meat" and "knife" straightened out. We got "grain" and "bowl" confused for a while, but it came clear. "Eat" was easy. "Table" and "bench" could be illustrated. "Gun" was my and Pegleg's laser guns. "Sling" designated the simple, pliant pair of thongs and leather cup wrapped like a strange flattened reptile around San's right forearm. "Stones" bordered the pathway by which the table sat. San's slanted eyes gleamed as he slipped a rock from his ammo bag, held it up, and said, quite plainly, "Stone."

It was interesting—it always is—how quickly the weird appearance of the towering, skeletal slingman sort of seemed to metamorphose as we became more familiar with each other. We noticed his differences less and less. As we worked on the speech he became just another man, working with us toward a common goal. And a good sharp man, at that. I felt proud of my different fellow human. For that he was human I hadn't doubted from the first. True human. Earth-human. But if I had known what I'd go through to check out my conviction, I doubt if I would have been that curious.

We left our utensils on the table. I presumed that this was a chief's prerogative. We "walked" along the "path." Each shelter we passed was a "house." Sometimes a "man" stood by the "house," sometimes a "woman." Both kinds passed us on the "path."

The "house" we stopped before differed in no detail that I could see from the others of the settlement. But on the rough wall by the entrance was a 10 × 18 photograph of the *Stardust,* with Cap'n Jules Griffin and a couple of his engineers standing by an open port. This was San's house.

A tall blue woman emerged from the doorway. Her still, cold, expressionless face turned first to San, then to us. It might have been molded from smooth blue plastic. The slitlike blue eyes did not seem to blink. I forgot—or I did not notice—her lack of clothing, her lack of curves, her lack of everything that makes a woman beautiful. For this gal had it. She was regal.

The kicking infant in her long arms practically stopped my breath for a minute. He was blue, sure, a nice delicate pale shade, but he was an Earth baby. Chubby, roly-poly, all the descriptive words you use about a well-fed, hearty baby. His eyes were round and solemn, his well-shaped head was covered with dark fuzz. He didn't smile, but he looked just ready to. And he chirped and gurgled and drooled like any five-month-old that ever grew under Earth's yellow sun.

"Maybe I *ought* to give up geology," Pegleg said. "Boy, did I call it on the button this time!"

"You're a credit to science," I agreed. "Look at Papa!"

I have commented repeatedly on the lack of expression, the coldness, the stillness of those skull-like blue faces. San, though, had learned to smile. He was breaking the ancestral pattern. It was as though long-dormant emotion was finally beginning to crack through his grim, frozen facade. For the look he bent on his plump, squirming son was nothing less than fatuous. There was a proud father!

He placed long fingers gently on the gaunt shoulder of his impressive woman. He looked at us and smiled. "Del!" he said.

Her unblinking eyes regarded us like an entomologist looking at a speciman. Still, my hide is tough. I took a step forward, held out my hand and smiled.

"Del!" I said. "Friend!"

She flicked a cold glance at her husband's unprecedented smile, then back to me. Deliberately she shifted the baby to one arm, reached the other hand to grasp mine. Her face softened. It wasn't a smile; it was dignified recognition of my presence. She was first lady in this settlement, the chief's lady, and I had a strong impression that she wasn't about to let anybody forget it.

"Osco!" she said clearly. "F'iend!"

She knew who I was. She knew which was which, and she remembered our names. I would have bet that San had to make a complete report each evening before she'd let him sleep.

She faced Pegleg with the same aloof graciousness, called his name, grasped his hand and said "F'iend!" San positively beamed. He seemed to lose a little of the imposing assurance of the man in charge.

Pegleg got it just as I did. "Behind every successful man there is a drivin' woman," he said. "Hoo, boy!"

"A vile calumny," I retorted. "Inaccurate, unfair, and maintained in a preservative compounded largely of sour grapes."

Our polite smiles had become grins, and if Del didn't detect the change, she wasn't the woman I thought she was. Still, she couldn't understand us, so the asides were safe for a while, anyhow.

"Make over little Rollo there," Pegleg suggested. "Even she won't be proof against that."

San beat us to it. He touched the baby with a long blue finger, and the little fellow promptly grasped it.

"Dan!" his father said proudly.

"Dan!" I said gently. I bent close to the round-eyed Prince of Wales, or the Hadornian equivalent, and chucked him under his drool-slick little chin. He regarded me steadily, and suddenly he grinned. It was genuine, happy, spontaneous. All he'd needed was something to imitate.

"Ay-ee!"

His mother's astonishment was real. Little Dan's grin was the first baby smile that had ever happened on this planet, I suppose. Certainly it must have been millennia since the last one, at least. Del looked at us, then back at her offspring's wide, toothless mouth. Her painted eyebrows lifted. Her cold, slitted eyes widened. For a minute it seemed a tossup as to whether she would decide for the traditional or the progressive. Then her own lips widened, and she smiled back at her infant.

"And that's our good deed for the day," Pegleg said. "Every kid should know and remember his mother's smile. It's—it's only human!"

Chapter 7

At the end of another hour, we weren't sure that we had learned anything more. We hadn't been invited into a shelter; hadn't even had a glimpse inside. There were a couple of thatched arborlike structures, thirty or forty feet long, open on all sides, with benches and tables out of the weather. Apparently these were where people met and talked and socialized. As in the cooking glade, they came and they went, and since their faces showed no expression whatever, there was no way of telling why they were there or what they talked about. They all looked at us with cold intentness. None approached us, or seemed to feel that we were any direct concern of theirs.

San was our host. Probably this was why everyone stayed aloof. Away from Del and the heir apparent, he was again the chief on every count. And he was doing exactly what we were: learning all he could, picking our brains. He recognized communication as the essential step, so he worked at it. He soaked up English at a remarkable rate. He didn't forget, either. Of his tongue, we learned exactly one word.

"Ka?"

Again and again he pointed and repeated that single syllable, pitching his voice high. No doubt it meant "What is that?" or "How do you say it?" or whatever question would be appropriate. We tried pointing and saying "Ka?" to him, but he wouldn't buy it. He'd brush it aside. He'd point back to us, say "Ka?" himself, and insist on having the English of it.

The blue sun was slanting toward the Hadornian west.

"I always hate guests who stay too long," Pegleg said. "Shouldn't we be saying *'auf wiedersehn'* or something, and getting out of here?"

"Don't mix him up," I said. "One language at a time. Let's ask him where Lindy is. That'll get the idea across."

We didn't have to. The tall chief's face lighted at the name. He raised a long finger and one of the original guides came foward. They had stayed with us, silently, unobtrusively, keeping in the middle distance.

"Lindy!" San said. He followed the name with several crisp words. The fellow left swiftly.

A deep blue shadow drifted slowly along the ground toward us. The blue people made no sounds, but they froze wherever they were. Somehow, each man we could see had unwrapped his sling, and a stone was in the leather.

The scoutboat cruised silently, a hundred feet up, a slender, featureless cigar. I knew what the story was. We hadn't brought communicators with us. The jeep was equipped, of course, but it was across the river. Johnny Rasmussen was having us checked.

"Okay, Roscoe?"

The voice beamed down to us, trained on me, amplified and clear, but closely focused. It wouldn't alarm anybody. Ten feet from me no one could even hear it.

I waved my arms and made an all-satisfactory sign. The scoutboat moved on.

San had frozen like everyone else, but his sling was still on his arm. His skull-like visage was devoid of expression. He watched the boat, then flicked his cold eyes to me. His thin lips barely moved.

"Ka?" he asked.

Pegleg chuckled aloud.

"I knew it! You'll never have a better student, Dr. Kissinger! Make the most of it!"

"Scoutboat," I said to San. "Scoutboat."

San stretched to the limit of his great height, swept a leveled finger across the sky.

"Scoutboat!" he said.

The citizenry around us relaxed silently. Stones returned to ammo bags; slings were rewrapped on bony forearms. The quiet moving along the paths and in and out of shelters resumed. We could hear terse, brief talk. It was like the chicken yard after the hawk had gone over.

Until she came into view, I didn't realize that my subconscious had been nagging me about Lindy. I knew she was safe—but, as I often told her, she *was* the only woman I had. And, I might have added, the only one I was ever likely to want.

She waved from fifty feet away. "Hi, San!" she called.

The tall chief raised his long arm and smiled. "Lindy!"

The high-pitched voice that all blue people used was being deepened, lowered, as San imitated us. The lower tones seemed more compatible with English.

"Lindy . . woman," San said to me. "Osco woman."

"Correct!" I said heartily. "Roscoe, Lindy. San, Del."

"Ay-ee!" The chief had the relationship straightened out. He grasped Lindy's hand, said "F'iend," and they smiled at each other. They had genuine, mutual respect. The tall slingman who had been dispatched to bring her stopped some yards away with his fellows. He made no move to join the party.

San felt the importance of his role as host. A thought seemed to strike him. His bleak face suddenly became anxious.

"Lindy—eat!"

She understood. "I've eaten, thank you," she said. "Some unappetizing-looking gook in a wooden bowl. It was pretty good, though. Mel brought it in."

San's face cleared. "Mel, Lindy, eat?" The voice went up.

"Ay-ee!" my wife said solemnly.

"Good!"

I must have been saying that for the last couple of hours when he pronounced something well, but it was startling to have him use it. I could already recognize that our days of uncensored asides were numbered. San had made up his mind to speak our tongue. And what that boy decided, he did.

I motioned in the direction of the river. I pointed to Pegleg, to Lindy and to myself.

"Home," I said. *"Stardust."* I took a few steps in the direction I'd pointed, then returned, held out my hand.

"Good-bye," I told the chief.

He stared steadily. He was puzzled.

Lindy also walked toward the river, returned to say "good-bye." San's bleak eyes flickered. Then suddenly he turned to Pegleg, offered his long fingers.

"Good-bye!" he said plainly. Then he smiled. Oh, he was sharp!

Brief words to our guides sent them off down the path. We followed. A hundred feet away Lindy turned, waved, called "Good-bye, San!"

The chief raised his long arm one last time. "Good-bye!" His tones were deep. Then he turned and strode majestically away in the direction of his shelter.

"Stout fella," Pegleg said. "Henpecked, all right, but not beyond a well-defined point, I bet."

We made one more impression when again we were across the river. Our smoothly paddled dugouts eased up to the same piers they had left from hours before. Fifty yards away, up the trampled, hardened beach, the jeep sat as we had left it. So Pegleg did his jeep trick.

He took the remote control switch from his pocket, held it up on the palm of his hand. With a finger he manipulated it delicately. The jeep woke up, vibrated softly, then came toward us at a cautious ten miles an hour. I've often mentioned how much smarter it seems when Pegleg's not in it.

Our honor guard of tall slingmen gave way as the jeep came clanking up. Their still, bony faces didn't change. Each pair of slitted eyes was wider, though. If I could have known what they were thinking, it would have helped my understanding of them considerably. For I'd already begun to suspect that they had no concept of things supernatural. I doubted if ghosts, devils or magic had any part in their thought world. What was left, I wasn't sure.

We climbed aboard, Pegleg swung the jeep, and we rumbled away. Lindy looked back and waved. And from the clump of slingmen a forest of long arms sprouted. Then every man turned, suddenly and with finality. By their actions we had ceased to exist.

We followed our track exactly, to smash as little grain as possible. I plucked the ripest head I saw and we examined it as we rattled and swayed along. No matter how advanced our technology, I'll bet they never made tracks that are smooth to ride.

"This is the main ingredient in the vegetable pots," I pointed out. "Probably their food staple. Hence the specialized grain carts, the violent reaction to the grain birds. Without this crop, they might find the living hard."

"Too simple," Pegleg said. "There's enough getting ripe in this one field to last that village twenty years. It goes on for miles. And how'd they plant it? What keeps the weeds out? Et cetera."

"If I knew all the answers, we could leave," I said dryly. "Our work would be finished. That's what we're here for."

"Well, so it is," Pegleg chuckled. He likes to nag me. "However, they're your problems. I got rocks and strata and all kinds of fascinating stuff to look into. Can't waste my time with a bunch of blue savages."

"He's still touchy because the dancing-girls didn't pan out," Lindy said. "Rocks are a retreat from reality."

"Those the slingmen use are pretty real," I said. "Shouldn't we have the forcefield on? Because I'm fairly sure I can guess the answer to one of your questions. This field is a communal enterprise. It probably feeds a dozen villages."

Pegleg pushed the button and the dull red-black of the little light glowed.

"I'm ornery, but not stupid," he observed. "A very good point. San's people know us, but strangers might use us for target practice."

"Right! This is likely to be San's territory, but we don't know it. The map boys will have this whole sector photoed by now. The villages will be easy to spot. Then we'll know what the local situation is."

Pegleg increased speed to maximum. We made a little better time, but the track was no boulevard, and you couldn't have called our progress exactly a joyride. Still, the real experience is to ride the jeep in the open, when Pegleg has wheels on it. That really tests your fitness to survive.

The jeep communicator buzzed and rattled and experimentally cleared its throat. "Dr. Roscoe Kissinger, Dr. Linda

Kissinger, Dr. Williams! Dr. Rasmussen requests the pleasure of the company of all senior directive staff at dinner
tomorrow, Hadorn plus four. Appetizers at 1800 hours.
Don't let them sit down without you!''

Stony always fixed his own addendum to a communiqué. I
thought this was one of his weaker efforts.

''Oh, me,'' Lindy said. ''What a time to go formal! I think
I'll wear an apple-green sheath, white violets in my hairnet,
and my Malodorian pearls.''

''You can get away with anything, my dear, but won't that
take some getting used to?'' (I might mention in passing that
Malodorian pearls are blood-red.)

''I'm sticking out my tongue at this miserable blue light,''
Lindy said. ''I hope everyone dresses like a rainbow.''

The dinner invitation was a regular Rasmussen gambit.
We were used to it. The setup was crushingly formal—and
maybe Johnny has a point. He reminds us periodically that as
far as we know, we are the most highly civilized, most
knowledgeable organisms in the galaxy. He reminds us the
same way he reminds himself: he makes us dress for dinner.

I think it's good. In the field our attire ranges from rough to
practically nothing, and when we've been out a while it's
hard to tell who is studying what. Some of us gradually come
to look worse than anything we find. Johnny checks us up.

The dinners have other purposes, too. They are often
followed by a ''social hour,'' which usually becomes in
effect a series of staff planning meetings before it's very old.
Everybody's there. An invitation is just that, but nobody
skips those dinners. Sometimes they're dull, but they're
where things happen.

This one meant that field parties would be coming in. We'd
get a chance to talk to Merani about the massive architectural
remnants—the buildings, or whatever they were. The blue
men knew all about those buildings. I wanted to know their
connection with them. Lindy wanted to see them because she
wanted to go. You won't find a better reason than that.

Chapter 8

I proudly held the chair for Lindy. Then I went to my own seat a little farther up toward the head of the long table. Johnny has placecards at those dinners of his, and he pays no attention whatever to marital bonds. The seating shifts from dinner to dinner. Always our chief has some devious reasons for the arrangements he makes, but I often wouldn't hazard a guess as to what they are. I know only that everything he does has purpose.

We were all at our places when he came in and stood behind his chair at the head of the table. Tall, slender, his lean face smoothly tanned, his moustache waxed to needle points, his dinner jacket a marvel of good tailoring. He wore two decorations below his left jacket pocket. One was the jeweled swirl of the Galactic Medal for Extraordinary Achievement in Space. Only seven of them exist. (I try to wear my own with becoming modesty.) The other was a simple three-inch fragment of red ribbon held in place with a small gold pin. I've never known what it means—there are some things you don't ask Dr. Johannes Rasmussen.

He bowed slightly, showing his teeth in a correct, fleeting smile.

"Ladies and gentlemen!"

He swept the long table with his gaze, then, starting at his right, he named names. "Mr. Cheng, Captain Griffin, Dr. Julio, Dr. Kissinger, Miss Potts—" He went all around the curved length of the table, and when he got back to himself, he said, "I am delighted to have you here this evening. Won't you please be seated?"

It was formula. He always did it the same way. Actually, the ladies were already seated, but the men stood until Johnny said his piece. Then chairs scraped, utensils clinked, and the volume of conversation built. We had plenty to talk about.

My ears picked up bits and fragments as I tried the soup.

"—unusual plant variety in what ought to be tundra. We pressed forty-three numbers in two hours."

"—three hundred-mile cruise. Seven grainfields, thirteen villages, no grazing animals at all. What you think, Jim?"

"—steady, flowing cold air mass spilling on a wide front down those blue icefields—"

"—no other people. The slingmen freeze when a scout-boat goes over, and a lot of times we miss 'em. My pics show nine parties we never saw—"

"There are other people. Slingmen did not carve the buildings. And the buildings are used. This I now know."

Bud Merani sat across the table from me. He was bringing Pegleg up to date. Neither had touched the soup. I don't understand people like that.

"You hear that, Roscoe?" Pegleg saw that I was listening. "Bud says the amphitheater is inhabited. And not by slingment. Sound reasonable to you?"

I looked at Merani's small, dark intense face. "The first sounds believable," I said. "The other—well, you forget I haven't been there. But the slingmen are everywhere within five hundred miles, and nobody's even seen other men at all. That means something."

Merani nodded. "That is true. But the slingmen build only boats and shelters. And these buildings, these carvings—they are not only elaborate—they are now! They are current."

I spooned up soup. It had a tantalizing flavor, and I was hungry. "There's no other evidence of the stone carvers," I pointed out. "Find me another city. Catch me a builder. How could they live?" I shook my head. "Not enough evidence, Bud."

Pegleg nodded agreement. "Remains don't require an economy—a living culture does. Makes sense."

"Nonetheless," Merani insisted, "there are dwellers in the buildings. The doors are locked, the windows opaque, and to force entry would require destruction. We don't wish this. But we'll get in."

I went back to my soup. "Not until tomorrow," I said. "Why don't you fellows drink your soup? I'm sending my compliments to the chef."

Merani surveyed the ornate bowl before him with distaste. "The soup is blue! For forty hours I have been out in that blue light. I return on the chief's invitation and am served blue soup! It is too much." He pushed away the bowl. "I will wait to see the color of the meat."

As it happened, the meat was red. Good rare roast beef, oozing with fragrant juices. The little dark man tackled it with gusto.

Pegleg grinned at him. "With your background," he said maliciously, "I don't see how you can eat that. I thought cows were sacred."

Merani cut himself a luscious bite and tucked it in. "Nothing is sacred anymore," he mumbled tranquilly. "Protein is protein. But some tastes better than other. I am making up to my ancestors for ten thousand years of deprivation."

Now, there was a point of view I could go along with. My ancestors hadn't been deprived, so far as I knew, but I love food just the same. My thick body requires plenty of fuel. I suppose I'll be a fat old man, but I won't look back with regret on missed chances to eat.

Beside me, Ursula Potts was putting it away like a lumberjack. Little, skinny, with her witch's face and cold pale eyes, she was a most unlikely member of the Gourmet's Club of the Galaxy. But she loved to eat as well as I do.

"Well, Ursula," I said now, "what are the omens? What are the signs and symbols? Are the slingmen human? Are the building carvers still among us? How say you?"

Ursula looked at me pityingly. She wiped the grease from her thin lips. "Human," she said. "Earth-human." She dipped into her salad. "Don't know about the carvers. Have to see the place first."

"Why do we work?" Pegleg asked. "Why do we toil and sweat and beat our brains? We have a shortcut. Ask Ursula!"

Other than Lindy and me, I suppose Pegleg was the only one who could have got away with a crack like that. But we've had some strange times together, the four of us. So

Ursula continued to eat. "Optional." Her sharp voice was almost bland.

I used my most placating tone. "Ignore him, Ursula. I need help as well as support. Nobody really believes the blue men came from Earth. Nobody, that is, but me and you and, oddly enough, Pegleg. Give me data."

Ursula licked her fork. "Got none. Just feel it. Has to be."

She's said that to me a hundred times. And every time I've discounted it, I've been sorry. There aren't witches—I know there aren't. But if there aren't, how do you explain Ursula?

The dinner clinked and rattled and chattered on, just as its numerous predecessors always had. Dressed up, the diners were a colorful group. The women wore exotic gowns, experimental hairdos, jewelry from expensively grand to barbaric. My Lindy's Malodorian pearls glowed like blood spots across the scenic splendor of her discreetly sheathed bosom. Her giggle cut through the murmur and rumble of conversation. Just hearing it, I felt good.

The men wore dinner jackets. Black tie. I know that sounds strange. Antediluvian As far as Johnny Rasmussen is concerned, fads come and go, but the dinner jacket goes on forever. Though his name wouldn't tell you, his ancestry is rooted deep in a cluster of rocky little smudges off the coast of Europe. He's Victorian English to the depths of the soul that he doubts he has.

The desserts came and were appreciated. I caught Rasmussen's eye as the brandies were being set around, and the good strong aroma of coffee took over.

"Good feed, Johnny!" I said.

He didn't bend, though I know him like my own brother. Better—I haven't got a brother.

"I'm glad you enjoyed it, Dr. Kissinger."

"For the next one, I've got a request."

"Of course." He didn't crack, but he looked interested.

"I'd like to bring a couple of friends."

Johnny's eyes gleamed with amusement. Since most of our friends not already present were a hundred-plus light-years away, he knew what was coming.

"They will be welcome."

Keep the faith! Never lose poise! Always be gracious!

Johnny really believed these things. And he made them work.

"San and Del," I said.

Johnny grinned briefly, his teeth barely showing under his moustache. Everybody at our end of the table stopped talking to listen.

"I repeat, they will be welcome. But would it be—well, the kindest thing? They might feel, shall we say, out of place."

"And again, they might not." The whole table was listening now. "San's the boss in this neck of the woods. When he says 'frog,' everybody hops. Of course," I added seriously, "he almost certainly hasn't got a dinner jacket."

Johnny played it deadpan. "We would excuse him. And what about the lady?"

"Don't waste apprehension on Del. She'll be doing you a favor to come. With no beads atall, she'll be snootier than anyone here present with three strings! She knows her place—it's on top."

The whole guest list murmured.

"He's not kidding, Johnny," Pegleg cut in. "You've got to see her to believe her."

Rasmussen pushed back his chair and rose to his feet. "I'll certainly give us all the pleasure," he assured us. "Shall we adjourn to the lounge?"

In small groups we made the transition leisurely, full of good food and contented with the prospects of stimulating work ahead. In the lounge there'd be cigars and liqueurs in variety. We could pick each other's brains, plan, or just plain loaf. It was a good evening, but the most momentous decision had been made in the dining room.

Chapter 9

The next day I spent hours going over the geographers' pix of our general part of the planet. They had done a swift and a mighty good job, just as we had used good judgment in picking a base. We could hardly have done better if we had had maps ahead of time.

There were a few surprises. The mountain range was actually a series of ranges; a vast, rugged, jumbled blue wilderness. Some of it looked incredibly desolate and repelling. Great ice sheets thrust gleaming tongues down the sides of the higher peaks and they welded into a greater sheet that extended for hundreds of miles, apparently sheathing an entire interior plateau in a perpetual frozen shell. If there had been normal light, what a magnificent view it would have been!

It's our custom to pick a base and make studies in depth of a limited area. No explorer ship with the time schedule we allow ourselves could analyze an entire planet of any size. But it would survey, then spot-check and conclude. We'd had spectacular success doing just that.

We've never found a life planet of great size. Hadorn had perhaps the biggest dimensions we've explored, roughly an equatorial circumference of fifty thousand miles. That would take a lot of exploring. So our spot-check of the range and the plains to the west and a stretch of coast was going to have to be *it*. With the general information gathered from orbit, the radiation studies, Julio's analysis of the light situation, and Pegleg's data on the composition of the planet, we could put it together. We'd have a description. The Galactic Council couldn't ask for more.

I studied pix, thought, had a bourbon, had lunch, then called Cap'n Jules and had a scoutboat assigned to me. I had decided to do things in proper sequence for once. The geographers' photos had whetted my curiosity. I wanted to see for myself, to cruise low over cliffs and canyons and icefields, to look for breaks in the endless sweeps of dark, forbidding blue forests on the western slopes and among the foothills. I needed to make a pass over the plains between the forests and the ocean, to spot-check grainfields, to plot slingman settlements, to look for concentrations of wildlife. With our improved scoutboats I could do it from ten to a thousand miles an hour. As Ursula said, I could be a pioneer in comfort.

Lindy was working. Her staff was well into the culturing of hundreds of blue micro-forms, and some of them had her pretty excited. So far as I knew, Pegleg was also working. His composition studies were under way. The slightly less-than-Earth gravity of this vastly larger planet simply meant less density, of course, but he had to tell us why and how. But this was routine; his staff could do it. I suspected that he was cooking up an excuse to go back in to the amphitheater and heckle Merani and his team. After all, the carvings were his find.

I had a pilot assigned for the scoutboat. Otherwise, I was going alone. Of all the major researchers of the explorer ship *Stardust,* I'm the only one who has no staff; I do my own work. You can't get people to help you think—and that's my job. I don't collect, don't capture things, don't culture organisms. I take pictures, but others do it better. I analyze, and everybody's data is grist for my mill.

Just the same, I didn't go alone. When I boarded the scoutboat, Pegleg was leaning back comfortably in the other observation seat. "I knew you wouldn't mind," he grinned. "I called Cap'n Jules and he said you were going out."

"Feel free," I said, "so long as you're going where I'm going."

"Let me guess. Overview. Village counts. Low over the foothills. Maybe a pass at the amphitheater, just to be sure the whole thing isn't a hoax." He can read my mind.

I gave the word to the pilot, the port opened, and we eased silently out of our slip and drifted like a wraith above the grainfield.

"Business first," I said. "I want to see the grainfield pattern and the village arrangement for two hundred miles north and south of San's bailiwick. Get us high enough to see the ocean, and cruise at about a hundred. Can do, Pete?"

"Can do," the pilot said.

He was a youngster, but a whiz at his job. He usually took me out. Like Pegleg, he knew how I worked.

To see the ocean took us up ten thousand feet. Too high. I oriented myself, then brought us down to a thousand. We swept in twenty-mile circles, looping north. I dictated notes. The automatic cameras snapped away, a wide-field shot every thirty seconds and an occasional zoom shot as I directed. We swung low over San's settlement. As usual, the blue people froze into an immovable tableau. Then I saw one man stride out into an open space and raise a long arm upward. It had to be San.

I aimed the microphone, and my voice went down to him in a closely focused cone of sound. "Hi, San," I said. "Roscoe. Friend."

He stood immobile for a long minute, then slowly waved the long arm. I had the telescope zoomed on him by then and could see his lips move.

"Osco! F'iend!" he must have been saying. He didn't know he couldn't be heard.

He watched us for almost a circle, then turned with the abrupt finality they always showed and strode back among the trees.

As we suspected, four additional villages shared our grainfield. None was as large as San's settlement, and all were on smaller tributaries of "his" river. All were in groves of the metallic appearing trees, and looked identical in every way that I could check.

It might have been thirty or forty miles to the next grainfield. In between lay brushy land, patches of tall forest, and what appeared to be grassland. We brought the scoutboat low over these. Anything moving was easy to see. And the herbivores which I knew had to be present were there. They herded, like all the plant eaters of any size I ever saw.

These really did have size. We dropped down on the first band we saw, and I counted them. Thirty-one individuals. I guessed eighteen to twenty feet long, barrel-bodied, short-legged, with blunt, thick tails and huge heads. To graze they tipped their heads sideways, sweeping a flexible neck back and forth. I remembered then that the "grain birds" used that same odd approach to their food. These things continued to graze, always with the same side of the head next to the ground. I had activated the action cameras, and we barely drifted as we filmed them. I could study behavior and form at leisure in my lab.

"I'm just a poor rock-man," Pegleg said, "but I have random smatterings of other fields. If those varmints are wild, and this is a reasonable assumption, the predators that must have developed to feed on them are bound to be nothing you'd want for pets."

I zoomed up the binoculars I was using. The blue light glistened and rippled from their blue hides as the great creatures lumbered slowly along, ceaselessly swinging their vast heads. I could see why they glinted. They were scaled.

"Could be," I said. "Doesn't have to be, though. Food alone could be the limiting factor. Maybe their neck muscles wear out. Just one of the many problems it'll be fun to explore."

I had to discipline myself sharply, else I'd never have got farther than the plain and forest country. We checked two more grainfields, each with blue villages. Then we rose high and headed eastward toward the jumbled foothill country and the high-piled ranges beyond.

Pegleg was happier. Now the cameras were clicking for him as well as for me, recording the lines of uplift, the breaks, the faults, the raw escarpments, the deep-gouged canyons, the glacier-scrubbed high valleys—all the signs and sights that to the geologist add up to history. Naturally, I was more interested in the present, but the story of the blue men undoubtedly was tied up with that history.

I knew what I was looking for in the foothills and broken country. Man! Anything man-made, any evidences of human activity, of human occupancy. And they weren't there—nary a sign. Just mile on mile of endless blue wilderness.

Thin lines cutting and weaving and crisscrossing through

the vegetation became game trails when we dropped lower. Evidently there was life in plenty. I kept the action cameras going. I do much of my field work from an easy chair in my lab. Great stuff, photography! I could only hope that the frantic work in the photo lab to adjust film and equipment to Hadorn's blue light had been completely successful. Actually, I wasn't worried. Like all *Stardust* personnel, they knew their jobs. The geographers had had no trouble with their pix.

At the western edge of the first line of really rugged peaks, great cliffs flashed blue above the foothills, as though a tremendous fault line lay there.

"Once upon a time," Pegleg said, "the quakes along this range would really stir your coffee! Everything west of the range has dropped."

Since it was my trip, he made never a suggestion as to direction, but now his eyes pleaded like a puppy's.

"Swing in tight along the cliff line, Pete," I directed. "Then cruise slowly. Might as well look closely, and kodak as we go."

"Thank you, sir," Pegleg said. "You have a heart of gold."

"In memory of all the times I've used your jeep, I could do no less," I said kindly. "It's only fair to add, though, that I was going to do it anyhow. I need to see how the canyons cut through."

"Contraction," Pegleg said. "The canyons probably started as deep cracks. Then erosion and weathering gave them their present forms."

A cliff face ahead seemed subtly different from the ones we'd passed. It was darker, duller, and as I watched it seemed to shift, to ripple.

"Gor blimey!" Pegleg zoomed his binoculars on it. "What a mess! Will you kindly get all your nasty critters off of my nice rocks? Have a look, Roscoe. These are really nightmares!"

I had an inkling before I focused my glass. "So that's where they live," I said. "It figures, when I think of it. Those are old acquaintances, Dr. Williams. They're probably the number-one enemies of the blue men's economy. Those are what I call the 'grain birds.' And now I see why San and his boys were so ferocious in destroying them.''

You've seen the dark rows of cormorants lined up on the rocky crags of their nesting cliffs and islands along Earth's North American Pacific coast—or maybe you haven't. But that's what came to my mind. The cliff face before us was scarred with breaks and ledges, and on them the grain birds perched and clung in countless thousands. It was obviously a roost. No young could have survived the endless shifting, the beating of great wings, the shoving for position, the occasional savage assault of bird on bird.

Pete cruised the scoutboat along steadily, a hundred feet from the cliff face, a thousand feet above the piled and tumbled boulder fields, the vast tongues of talus and trash that lay along the base of the escarpment. And the inevitable happened. The "birds" saw us.

"Forcefield, Pete," I directed. "I hardly expected that we'd be quite so much of a sensation."

We were, all right. On the ground, in the grain, the "birds" had simply shown a defensive defiance when the blue men moved in on them. Apparently it was different when their particular airspace was invaded. They didn't hesitate. The thunder and swish of wings was like the roar of a train in a tunnel. A great fuzzy blue cloud, studded with bleak, gimletlike blue eyes and clashing rows of glittering blue teeth, rolled over the forty-foot scoutboat and blotted out the blue sun.

It was fantastic. They couldn't touch the scoutboat, of course, couldn't affect it in any way, but never should it be said that they didn't try. The forcefield held them a yard away from the hull, and every viewport was filled with evil crested heads and battering membrane-covered wings, each wing butt showing the curved, wicked blue talon. Everywhere you looked, it was a closeup in a horror film. We watched, and I had the action cameras recording it for posterity—and for my study report.

The "birds" couldn't hurt us, but they certainly did themselves no good. Fifteen-foot wingspreads require fifteen feet to operate, and the aerial traffic jam around the scoutboat was soon a bloody shambles. The ripping wing talons tore whatever they contacted. The chisel-toothed jaws snapped and chopped indiscriminately. The wing batter and roar never grew less, but the creatures made no vocal sounds at all. Apparently they were voiceless.

"Okay, Pete, shake 'em off," I said.

The scoutboat tilted upward, there was a pulse of power—and the viewports were clear. Two thousand feet below us a dense, milling swarm of tiny winged things swirled along the cliff face and out over the country beyond. They never even knew where we went.

We stayed high for a while, studying the way the canyons knifed into the range, and how the river systems spread and watered the open country. We circled and went south again. When San's territory and grainfield showed in the distance, we turned east into the mountains.

"Find your canyon," I said to Pegleg. "I've got sort of a hankering to lay eyes on those carvings. I've saved 'em for dessert."

We dropped lower, eased across the foothills, cruised close to great peaks capped with fresh blue snow. There was a maze of canyons, but Pegleg knew. It's hard to lose him. He pointed the way unerringly—and the canyon we followed bulged out ahead into a bulbous, hidden high-walled valley—the amphitheater.

The blue sun was lower than I'd have liked. Deep blue shadows half filled the valley, but the cathedral, at its farther end, was still bright. We drifted down, drifted in, and cruised in slow circles along the unbelievable walls.

They were hard to describe in my dictated notes and even here. Even the dozens of pictures that we took, from every height and every angle, don't give the impressions that the eye received firsthand as we drifted past buildings so elaborate, so ornate, and yet so gracefully designed and balanced that it was hard to conceive that they hadn't been constructed stone by stone. But we knew that they hadn't. Pegleg had discovered that, and Merani's archaeologists had verified it by careful examination. They were carvings on a scale impossible to envision even in terms of today's equipment and rock-working techniques.

"Pegleg," I said, "this is imaginary. It doesn't exist."

"Pretty solid imagination," Pegleg said. "First-line craftsmanship, I'd call it. Think of the work, Roscoe! Millions and millions of man-hours. And not a flaw."

The antigravity units that are basic in the scoutboats won't quite allow the crafts to hover, but they can be slowed to five or six miles an hour. We were drifting past a multi-storied edifice that might have been a public building, with great suites of offices and auditoriums and all manner of space inside. Or it could just as well have been a palace, with the ultimate in luxury for a royal family in residence, and ample room for hundreds of servants. Row on row of great wide windows looked with blind eyes out over the carefully trimmed and landscaped parkland of the amphitheater floor. Each window seemed to be curtained with rich, heavy drapery, a marvel of the sculptor's art.

"Roscoe!"

Usually Pegleg prides himself on taking things as they come. He can get annoyed, and frequently does, but never will he admit surprise. Well, almost never.

He had his glasses focused on the building slipping past, and he was actually trembling. "Swing around, Pete, and go past the palace again."

That showed how agitated he was. It was my scoutboat and my pilot. Only under stress would he have given an order.

"Third tier of windows, Roscoe. I think it was about above the big entrance arch. Watch the drapes!"

We cruised past again, watching intently. Nothing. Everything was dead, still, immobile, a picture in stone.

Finally Pegleg lowered his glasses. His narrow face was intent. His eyes gleamed. "Roscoe, how have you found my eyesight in the past? Pretty adequate, would you say?"

"Twenty-twenty," I agreed. "You can even see stuff that's none of your business."

"A drape was pulled back," Pegleg said. "A man was looking out. A blue man."

"A stone drape?" I said. "Come, now!"

Pegleg leaned back in his observation chair. "I was fussed for a minute there," he said, "but I didn't go blind. So we'll have to go with the obvious. Not all those drapes are stone."

I considered, looking out at the marvelous blue carvings slipping past, looking down at the obviously maintained park.

"It fits," I admitted. "There's life here. Probably much life. What, whence, whither—I hate to say it, but I guess that's Merani's job. Let's hail him."

I flipped a communicator switch. We had seen Merani's camp among the trees near the cathedral, and several of his team had waved as we drifted over.

"Hello, scoutboat! Merani here. Who is it—Pegleg?"

"And Roscoe," I said. "How's it going, Bud?"

"Baffling," Merani said. "Frustrating. This place is lived in, but we've seen nobody. We can't get in, but I'd wager my next beefsteak that some of those doors work."

"We bear glad tidings," I reported. "A blue man was watching us from a third-floor window. The drape was pulled back. The big palacelike structure about half a mile back, on the north wall."

"Ah-h!" Merani sounded vindicated. "That was going to be the next step. We have bounced the jumpers and tried to examine upper parts of buildings. Tomorrow we'll have climbing teams going up."

"Cover 'em from below," I advised. "I think you'll find a way in, but somehow I doubt you'll be welcomed. As Ursula would say, can't say why. Just feel it."

I could hear Bud chuckle. He's a cold-blooded little man. I doubt if he knows what fear is. He's always so interested and busy he hasn't time to think about it.

"We can take care of ourselves," he said.

"Could you carve these buildings?" I asked. "If they're hollowed out inside—even to a limited extent—the occupants are liable to be pretty special, aren't they? You may run into beings we've had no hint of before."

"Granted," Merani said. "But didn't you say you saw a blue man?"

"I saw him, Bud," Pegleg put in. "Just a fleeting glimpse, but I'd swear to him. Maybe the carver race is keeping him for a pet."

"I've seen only the blue men's pictures," Merani said. "But they don't look very pettable to me."

"Nor to me," Pegleg admitted. "Just hypothesizing, Dr. Merani. Just brainstorming."

"I have a question," I put in. "When you carve something, you make chips and rubble and dust. When you carve the granite walls of a valley four or five miles long, you ought to have the doggonedest rubble heap the mind of man can picture. Millions of tons of granite chips and fragments. Where are they, Bud?"

"Bright boy!" Merani's soft voice purred out of the communicator. "The point had occurred to us. I can tell you where to find a few tons. The walkways and trails all through the park are made of them. Large chunks have been used in piled artistic arrangements, to emphasize tree and shrub concentrations and the like. But not even a tiny fraction of a percent of what must have been removed. And if, as we are now convinced, tunnels or even more extensive space is hollowed out behind the bas reliefs, there'll be more millions of tons. I don't know, Roscoe. I know only the obvious. They are somewhere—and not too far away, I'd think."

"Wouldn't make sense," I agreed. "Still, I'm not too sure this valley makes sense. Keep plugging, Bud. You've just given us an assignment. We'll look for the tailings piles."

You can't land a scoutboat on the ground successfully. They're not designed for it, and once down they can't be launched again. But as long as they're airborne, they're versatile. With them I have scouted the narrowest valleys, circled peaks, followed streambeds. I've taken them between the trees in giant forests, and once, on the memorable investigation of Olympus II, Lindy and Pete and I cruised a hundred and fifty miles of connected underground caverns, never touched a wall, and got out safely.

We now rose from the amphitheater into the late afternoon rays of Hadorn's blue sun. A thousand feet above the valley rim we swung in slow circles, watching, searching, the wide-angle cameras clicking every thirty seconds. The surrounding country was all a part of an immense plateau, high, broken, with narrow cracks and fissures checking its surface and long walls of morainal rubble outlining where ice sheets of the past had scrubbed across it. Canyons with perpendicular walls and streams on their rocky floors led out of it. Over some parts of its area vast boulders lay in gargantuan piles and jumbles.

But it all looked natural—natural and ancient. In the farther distance, great blue peaks emphasized the igneous nature and geologic newness of the whole vast uplift system. But in terms of a living race, it was an old, stable landscape.

We circled and cruised and crisscrossed until the sun's rays were nearly level, and its cold blue disc appeared ready to slide down into the distant blue ocean. There were days of hard work ahead in the cameras and on the note tapes. I felt good about everything. Pegleg leaned back in his observation chair. He looked relaxed, satisfied.

And suddenly, as always after a long day in the field, the important things were Lindy, to kiss me and be glad I was back, to listen and be interested while I told about the day; a shower and good food, maybe preceded by a small libation from a bourbon bottle that had been filled in a little distillery back in the Tennessee hills a hundred light-years away. For all his achievements, concerns, and capacities, man is basically a simple animal in his needs and wants. And I am a simple man.

"Take her to the barn, Pete," I directed.

Promptly the little craft straightened out and flashed for the mother ship. At four hundred miles an hour it took only a few minutes. The grainfield rippled beneath us, the *Stardust* loomed, our port opened, and the little scoutboat eased into its slip. Young Pete had a woman of his own waiting for him. One of Lindy's technicians was the center of his world. He grinned at me as he cut the power. "Good day, Dr. Kissinger!"

"A fine day, Pete," I agreed. "And we had the best pilot on Hadorn. Thank you much."

I collected tapes and films, unloaded my own cameras and recorders. I always do. Then I know that everything is properly cared for, everything's done right. Assistants are fine, but they're human. I've never let myself down yet.

Chapter 10

Lindy was not in our quarters, so I put a call for her on automatic intercom. That would check her lab, check wherever else she might be, and notify her that I was back. Then I poured the bourbon and set it just outside the shower, where I could reach it from time to time.

After my muscles relaxed and my work tensions eased, I finished the shower with hard needle-streams of cold water. I toweled my way into the bedroom. My communicator was blinking green. I flipped the switch.

"Kissinger," I said.

"Stony, Roscoe. Your automatic on Lindy—she's not back yet."

"Didn't know she was out. Where'd she go, Stony? You're in contact, aren't you?"

There was a distinct pause before Price answered. "We were in contact until about an hour ago," he said reluctantly. "Then she cut out. Haven't heard anything since. I figure they left the jumpers, collecting, and haven't returned to them. They're probably okay, but I've notified Dr. Rasmussen."

"Who's 'they'?"

"Just Lindy and a technician. Barbara."

Barbara was the light of young Pete's eyes. In spite of me, I felt a little chill at the coincidence.

"Where were they at last contact?"

"They went south, diagonally out across the grainfield. Lindy was following a pollen stream, trying to track down the plants, which apparently she's not been able to identify. The pollen causes allergic irritations, I believe. The last check put them about thirty kilometers southeast. That's twenty kliks beyond the southeast corner of the grainfield."

78

"There's a blue village at that corner," I said. "The smallest one, I think. We've not contacted it yet. Did they mention it?"

"Don't know, actually. Ivan was on the console. I've just come into the com center. I'll check it out."

I stood watching the blinking yellow eye of the communicator. Automatically I finished toweling as I waited.

But the next voice wasn't Stony's.

"Rasmussen, Roscoe. I've reordered your scoutboat. Same pilot. His girlfriend is with Lindy. Pegleg will be there in a few minutes."

"Thanks, Johnny."

I didn't ask silly questions. Rasmussen's actions always told me what he thought.

"Dr. Hefflefinger will take another scoutboat. She was collecting in the general area yesterday, and may be helpful. Dr. Peters will take a squad of jumpers and proceed to the area of last contact. All will take your orders. I will stand by. Good luck, Roscoe!"

I wiggled the switch to show that I understood. Suddenly I didn't trust myself to speak. For years I've wondered if I really have premonitions or just a good imagination. Right now I had little doubt   something had happened to Lindy.

I was still dressing when Pegleg came in. He wore the same field clothes, an extra gun, and carried a large plastic bag. His narrow face was tranquil. He could have been on his way down to the corner to post a letter. "Came by the galley," he remarked, as I strapped on my own guns. He patted the bag. "Sandwiches. We may be out until after dinner."

I tried to imitate his nonchalance, but it was rough going. I picked up the bourbon bottle, tightened the cap, and handed it over. "Good idea," I said. "Put that in, too. We may need it."

Young Pete was sitting in the pilot's seat when we boarded. His face was serious, curiously still. Somehow he didn't look so young any more. But he looked capable, steady, dependable. He said nothing; just waited for orders.

"Late dinner after all, Pete," I said. "Take her out!"

The port opened, the scoutboat moved smoothly from its

slip and out into the blue dusk. Long shadows, cold and repelling, lay across the miles of grain. Far to the east, just above the tumbled, jagged silhouette of the range, the three blue moons of Hadorn had begun their tandem march across the cold blue sky.

A twin of our scoutboat was sweeping in slow circles around the prone *Stardust*. My communicator buzzed, blinked and cleared its throat.

"Winkie, Roscoe." It was a crisp, no-nonsense woman's voice. Dr. Winifred Hefflefinger would be my choice of all the field botanists who ever swung a plant pick. The habitat didn't exist that she wouldn't explore, and come out with her vasculums and presses bulging. "Winkie will collect plants along the route to Heaven," Pegleg said once, "and press 'em and dry 'em out by the radiance of the Pearly Gates."

"Glad you're there," I said. "You have the coordinates, Winkie. What's it like back there where they got the last message?"

"Good collecting," Winkie said. "I picked up thirty-one numbers in the broken country past the grainfield. Rough, though. Brushy. Full of little ravines. Whole mess of little blue varmints of all kinds zipping away. Lively."

"Any blue people? Any slingmen see you?"

"There's a village," Winkie said. "I'm sure you've mapped it. We jumped around it, and nobody followed us. I think the word is out everywhere about us now. But I wouldn't say we aren't watched."

"I wonder," I said. "Will you lead us in, Winkie? We'll circle and spotlight. It'll take Jim Peters a while to get there with the jumpers. Keep your communicator open."

Winkie's scoutboat straightened out and moved slowly away. We followed its radio beam. It wasn't actually dark, but the lack of contrast in the blue light made the terrain a jumbled mass of shadows. As the moons rose higher, we'd have better visibility.

In a few minutes the stream on which the blue village was located glittered below us. Then we were drifting on over the gloomy brushy country, on toward the dark hills. When Winkie gave me the word we used our magnaflash spotlights, swinging low and quartering a five-kilometer-square area thoroughly.

The zoologist jumper team was the ideal ground search party in a situation like this. A couple of Peters's field technicians were trappers and students of nocturnal life, and this was their kind of night. For that matter, they were all as antilight as owls. Even with increasing blue moonlight everything seemed much more multichromatic than it possibly could by day, and so, from our point of view, more normal.

Sooner than I expected, Jim Peters's voice broke out of my communicator. "We have your flashes, Roscoe. What's the M.O. for us?"

"You'd know better than I, Jim. I want the quadrat we're outlining searched for needles. Tracks, the abandoned jumpers, anything at all. I'm the inside scoutboat. Winkie will outline."

"Roger. Point if you see anything. George Wildcat is with us. If he can't track on Hadorn, it'll be another first for this planet. Any comment, George?"

"Can do." The Indian's soft voice was laconic.

"Find her for me, Wildcat!" I probably sounded like a desperate child. And, while I was functioning normally and calmly, down inside I *felt* desperate. "Find her, and all the firewater your skin can hold is yours for life!"

"Ugh!" the Indian said. "We'll find her. But firewater bad for Injun, or for bad Injun—I never remember which. Better make mine a chocolate ice cream soda, Dr. Kissinger!"

Good boy! I grinned across at Pegleg, and he winked. The Wildcat rarely said ten consecutive words, but he felt my need and went along. We've got a good bunch! Come to think of it, I never met a really bad field man. I like 'em all.

Pete swung the scoutboat at its lowest speed back and forth across the quadrat. Pegleg and I operated searchlights while Winkie drifted steadily around the area, her spotlight flashing at intervals. And down on the ground the jumper team deployed as Jim Peters directed. Tiny pinpoints of light flashed as the youngsters sifted the landscape through a sieve. But I found it.

My light swept across a small area completely bare of vegetation. A jumper frame sat in the middle of it. I held on it, Pegleg's light joined mine, and Pete turned the scoutboat in the tightest circle possible. The pinpoints converged on the flooded spot.

"Got it, Dr. Kissinger!" It was the Wildcat's soft voice. "Cut off your searches."

We switched off. The pinpoints hopped about like fleas with flashlights. Then Jim Peters: "Two jumpers, Roscoe. No collecting gear at all, so they were parked. The girls were working the area for specimens. This is all we need. Stand by."

Stand by we did, but it was rough. We watched the tiny flashes, and even Pegleg gnawed his fingernails. I had Pete increase our radius and we swept around in a wide ellipse. Finally Jim cut in again. "This isn't good telling, Roscoe. Things are pretty smudged up, but it looks like they went northeast, into the foothills." He seemed to hesitate. "They had company. Blue men, a whole squad. Five or six, anyway. They were probably carried."

I don't think I had considered this. Accident, likely. Wild animal predators, possibly. Poison plants, believable. But kidnap? From what I had seen of the blue men, that wouldn't be their way. They'd use those deadly slings. Further, I was pretty sure they all knew about us, knew stones couldn't hurt us, knew about the strange, bright rays. Something wasn't right.

"Where'd they come from, Jim? Any hint?"

I didn't see how they could find anything down there in the shadowy, cold blue dark, but they were doing it.

"Not from the nearby village. Apparently nobody from there came close." Again Jim seemed to hesitate. "From the north, Roscoe. The boys agree. They came in fast and they came direct. They knew what they were doing. They came to do what they did."

From the north. That would be—I stared at Pegleg. His close-set eyes were as cold as anything in this blue land. I knew he had got it before I did.

"San!" he said.

It went through me like a chill, and I shuddered. San! The

only village north for many miles was San's village. The others around our grainfield were west, toward the ocean.

"He liked her," Pegleg said.

It wouldn't wash. I knew it wouldn't. I wouldn't believe it. "So does everybody," I said.

"Everybody isn't a chief," Pegleg said. "A chief who gets what he wants."

I was glad Pegleg was saying it, glad I was hearing it with my ears. Because it sounded wrong. It was reasonable, but when he spoke the words I knew I wasn't believing them. But there *was* a point. San would know.

"Are you getting this, Jim?"

"Loud and clear."

"So?"

"This is the Wildcat's meat, Roscoe. A squad of eight-foot men won't lose him, no matter what. And Jubal's almost as good."

"Often bettah!"

The African's deep voice had an English accent as crisp as Rasmussen's.

Even with the humming tension I could hear Jim Peters's chuckle, and the huge young black man's mellow laugh.

"Sorry, Jubal," Peters said. "No aspersions. We need you both." His tone changed. "We'll stay on it, Roscoe. We're prepared. If they go to San's village, we'll know by morning. I suggest you go back to the ship, rest, and keep in touch."

"Jim!" I was indignant. "It's my woman, remember?"

"And mine, Dr. Peters!" Our pilot hadn't spoken before, but there was no doubt of how he felt.

"Can either of you do anything we're not doing?" Jim Peters took charge. "You can't land the scoutboat, so you've got to go back. And if you jump out in this gloom, you'll break your fool necks! We'll need you in the light, Roscoe. But tonight it's our show."

"Right, Jim." Of course he was right! "Thanks." Thanks for taking hold when one of the best field men in the Galaxy loses his grip for a moment. Thanks for understanding. Thanks for boosting the pride of two young super-trackers so they'll be unbeatable, unlosable. Just thanks.

"We're going in, Winkie," I said to the open circuit. "Jim feels we've done our bit."

"Makes sense," Winkie said. "Don't worry, Roscoe. This is everybody's business now."

Never again will I say to a man in trouble, "Don't worry!" It's a stupid admonition. It really says, "Don't be human!" It usually comes from the best intentions, but it isn't smart. From now on I intend to say, "You *have* got problems! Let me give you a hand!" That's positive—and possible. "Don't worry" isn't.

Winkie's scoutboat lights dwindled. We followed, leaving the zoologists down in that crazy-quilt of jumbled terrain and dark blue shadows. They had sympathy for us, but *they* weren't worried. They were challenged, up on the step. They were having the time of their lives. And that was what consoled me as we eased into our slip and disembarked for the long night of waiting.

Part II

The Volloon

Chapter 11

The rattling purr of my communicator brought me out of it the next morning. I had thought over the situation and had taken a hypno. Knocked out, I figured I'd get some kind of rest; for when I left the ship again, I wasn't coming back without Lindy.

"Boy, you were under," Pegleg's voice jeered out of the speaker. "I thought for a minute that you'd hit yourself too hard."

"News, Pegleg," I urged. "Save the comment."

"Two items," Pegleg said. "One, the blue men came from San's village. Two, they didn't go back there. They veered east into the range, split up four different ways, and for all practical purposes vanished. You want it straight, you get it straight."

That was Pegleg. It doesn't do to irritate him, especially when he's as concerned and involved as I am myself. I wasn't feeling funny, but I grinned. "San, I suppose." I forced myself to say it.

Pegleg didn't answer for a space. "You don't believe it," he said finally. "No evidence either way, apparently. Jubal backtrailed the party to the village, but didn't think it too smart to pay a visit. San didn't have to be a part of the action at all."

I was getting into field gear, putting together a concentrated survival field pack.

"Anything that goes on in that village, San knows about," I said. "He may not have been a part of it, but he knows."

I could hear rustling and clinking as Pegleg threw his equipment together. I could see him as well as if he had been in the room. When he'd finished, his pack wouldn't differ

two items from mine. And I could bet that he knew exactly
where we were going.

"What San knows about, San condones," said Pegleg.
"Otherwise he'd stop it. He authorizes anything that goes
on."

"So far as we know," I qualified.

It was like a man talking to himself.

My breakfast appeared from the dispenser. I took time to
set it up properly and to eat without haste. I knew Pegleg was
doing the same thing. There was no reason for hurry, every
reason to get set up for the long, hard job. And it was going to
be a rough assignment, with a possibility of an ending we
didn't want to think about. We knew that, too.

"The Wildcat is working the best of the escape trails into
the mountains," Pegleg volunteered. I could hear him chew-
ing. "Two men, he says. The other trails have been marked.
He and Jubal will check 'em all, if need be. Jim has set up a
base camp about fifty miles in, along the escarpment line.
Jumper squads are fanning out from there. Rasmussen has
four scoutboats roving, watching and taking pics and serving
as communications relays."

I drank a third cup of coffee. That completed the nourishment. I tried the pack for feel, checked my laser guns, shook
everything into place. The communicator blinked and Stony
Price joined the conversation.

"Item, gentlemen," Stony said. "Report from Dr.
Merani. A slingman came up the trail into the amphitheater,
ran into a pair of the archaeologists, and tried to blow 'em
down with his sling. They were wearing reinforced belt
fields, so he had no luck. They bracketed him with rays, and
he gave up. Put on the same show they did the day you burned
the birds, Roscoe. Turned his back, put his arms in front of
his eyes and went catatonic. He could be one of the kidnap-
pers."

"They're holding him?"

"Ironed to a tree," said Stony cheerfully. "Much good
it's doing, though. He won't say a word, and nobody could
understand him if he did. Can you communicate at all? That's
what Bud wants to know."

"He can say 'Ka?' " Pegleg cut in. "San was so determined to learn English, he wouldn't let us learn anything.''

"San," I said dryly, "is very much the key. Ready, Pegleg? We'll stay in touch, Stony. We're jumping."

"Luck," said Stony. He's used to us.

Pegleg and I met a few minutes later on the jumper platform. Same field gear, same pack. The blue sun was already above the peaks to the east, and the blue grainfield around us rippled in the brightening blue light. It's interesting how you adjust. The strange blue landscape seemed almost normal. I remembered Lindy's horror when she first looked at me in the blue sun's rays, and remembering Lindy brought me grimly back to the job at hand.

"A straight line is the shortest distance between two points," I said. "Let's cut across lots."

I took a compass check, we blasted from the platform, soared, tapped, blasted, and soared. We went across the grainfield on a long diagonal, following that straight line. You can make time with a jumper if you put your mind to it.

The river showed in the distance. In a couple of minutes, we dropped down onto the hard-packed shore, where the stone docks provided mooring for the needle-slim dugouts. And there wasn't a boat on our side of the river. Not a slingman showed.

At the docks on the village side, the boats lay in rows. None were on the river. Blue men moved among the shelters, though. We were ignored, and that, while blue-man normal, wasn't right for the whole village. We should have been welcomed if all were well.

We stood in our jumper frames and considered. I watched the village with binoculars. The slingmen seemed not to be watching us, but they were.

"They know the story," Pegleg said. "I don't imagine we'll be greeted as 'F'iend' this trip."

The situation seemed clear enough, but still I watched and hesitated. The blue men weren't defying us. It wasn't an active agonistic display such as most primitives would put on. They just seemed to be hoping we'd go away.

"There's a catch, Pegleg," I said. "San's too intelligent—they're all too intelligent to pull a simple snatch like that. They know what we can do. They know the rocks bounce off us. They've seen the lasers and the light rays and the scoutboats going over. They have an idea of what the *Stardust* may be.''

"Now, that last I doubt," Pegleg said. "How could they?''

"Haven't the foggiest," I admitted, "but I think they do. We don't belong on Hadorn. We're here. Scoutboats fly. Why can't the *Stardust* fly?''

Pegleg raised his eyebrows. He followed me, but I explained anyway. "I'm thinking blue man," I said. "How else could they reason?''

"Keep thinking," Pegleg urged. "Tell me why no boats. With all that mobility, do they think we can't get across the river?''

"That's just a message," I suggested. "It says the welcome mat isn't out. It says please go 'way.''

"And leave them with their captives—their specimens!'' Pegleg's voice wasn't pleasant.

"Pegleg!''

It was a little nagging thought, but it wouldn't retreat.

"Say that again," I said. "There was an idea there somewhere.''

"You heard me," Pegleg said.

"I did. Let's find San. If he's here we'll give him some use for that English he knows.''

We tipped the jumpers, blasted, soared across the river and dropped gently onto the shore, just beyond the close-ranked rows of deserted boats. Then, one behind the other, we bump-rocked our jumpers up the path from the wharf. And the blue people finally admitted our presence. They stared, and their concern showed through the cold immobility of their skull-like faces.

I still couldn't tell one from another, so I accosted the first slingman close to the path.

"San!'' I said it curtly.

The tall man's long slits of eyes looked at me steadily. There was no expression on the blue face, but somehow he seemed to exude a sort of remote dignity. His sling was free in the skeletal right hand, but no stone was in the pocket. With a smooth movement he wrapped the sling around his forearm, deliberately turned his back, and slowly stalked away.

"I don't think he means 'Come along,' " Pegleg said.

"He doesn't. He means, very politely, 'Go to hell!' "

We stood there in our jumpers, egg rapidly accumulating on our faces. We knew he had spoken for everybody. It was our move. The one thing we couldn't do was nothing.

"Let's go walkabout," I said. "We'll at least leave no doubt as to what we want."

So we bump-rocked along the meandering trail, past and around shelter after shelter and finally, by luck, we came out into the cooking glade. I smelled the meat before we got there. There were people, both men and women, and they watched us come in silence. Then each turned, without haste, and followed the nearest path out of the glade. In a couple of minutes we had the scattered, glowing fires, the steaming kettles and the fragrant, spitted roasts of meat all to ourselves. We looked at each other.

"Keep moving!" I said. "I think I remember."

We followed the path we had taken with San, and when we came to his shelter I recognized it. It was like all the others, but I had made a point of the location. No *Stardust* picture on the wall now, but it was San's home.

It seemed deserted.

"Here's where we get rid of the hot potato," I said. "The insides of these things are private, taboo. We weren't invited in, remember? Neither was Lindy."

I stepped out of my jumper frame. "Cover me," I said. "This'll get action."

Slowly I walked the few yards from the path to the closed door of the shelter. I stood for a moment, then put up my hand toward the rough latch. I didn't have to touch it.

The door swung open toward me. San's tall woman stood almost against me, the cold perfection of her carved, still blue face somehow conveying outrage. On her arm the round-eyed heir apparent looked at me unblinkingly.

I retreated a step, recovered, then bowed slightly.

"Del!" I said. I didn't add "Friend." Hypocrisy had its place, I supposed, but this wasn't it.

She said nothing. We stood and locked gazes. After a minute, and I wouldn't have believed it, I had the better of it. Her regal dignity was all there, but there was something else. Without changing a muscle, she almost seemed to be pleading. I tried to make no sign.

"San!" I said coldly.

She tried to battle me for it, but the odds were all on my side, and she knew it. She turned her grim profile and spoke toward the interior of the shelter.

"San!"

To my astonishment the towering figure of the chief pushed past the woman and stood looking down on me.

"Osco!" he said. The cold blue face was inscrutable, unreadable.

"Where's Lindy, San?"

He misunderstood, or pretended to. He raised one skeletal hand, palm out.

"Lindy, Osco," he said. "Del, San!" His voice was deep.

I was baffled, but I worked on it. He knew what I was asking. He was playing "Let's Pretend." And he knew that I knew.

"Where is she, San?" I insisted. "Where's Lindy?"

He looked at me.

Suddenly I gestured toward the shelter, took a step forward. "Lindy there?"

He blocked me, held up the long hand palm out. "No!"

He'd learned that, I remembered, along with "good" and "see" and "walk."

I stared up into the slitted blue eyes, tapped my laser gun holster. "Gun!" I said. "Lindy—*ka?*"

He had watched the birds crisp up. He knew what I threatened. But he didn't wilt. Instead, the lines of his mask-like face slowly gave way to a grim smile.

"Osco, gun," he said, "Lindy—" He had no word to follow the name, but he drew the edge of his great hand across his sinewy throat. It was a universal gesture. Two could threaten.

I should have been raging. Behind me I could feel Pegleg's baffled anger. But San had quit pretending, so we were making progress. He was admitting it. He knew where Lindy was. I worked on that.

"Lindy, San, friends," I protested. "Lindy, *ka?*"

Before Lindy, facial expression had been almost totally lacking among the blue people of Hadorn. I'd bet that San's first smile, there in front of the *Stardust* days before, had been the first for his race for millennia. And, on our visit here, his face had become almost mobile. He had smiled, he had frowned, his slit eyes had widened with interest, had narrowed subbornly when he insisted on a word or a meaning. I watched his face now.

He puzzled me at first. Expression there was, but it meant nothing. He seemed perturbed, though. The grim positiveness of the threat he had made was a passing thing. Now his slit eyes avoided mine; his thin mouth became an almost invisible line; his hands clenched restlessly. If he had been an Earth-type man, I'd almost have said that he was uncertain; even that he was wrestling with his conscience.

Suddenly he spoke: "Lindy, *kantokar!*"

The tone was expository. It was also apologetic, and, I thought, almost a little indignant. I'd never been more frustrated in my life.

"Don't understand! No savvy! *Kantokar? Ka?*"

San wagged his long hairless head, looked around helplessly. Then his eyes fixed on Pegleg.

"Pe-leg. Stone. *Kantokar!*"

He bent, picked up several small stones, pantomimed placing them in a belt pouch. He watched me anxiously. I didn't get it.

He reached over to the nearest shrub, plucked off a cluster of blue leaves. "*Ka?*" he asked.

"Leaves," I said.

He handed them to me, motioned placing them in a pouch.

"Osco, leaves, *kantokar!*"

Pegleg's shocked voice fairly crackled. "We collect stuff, Roscoe. Stones, leaves, things like that. *He has collected Lindy!*"

"Easy, Pegleg. We're on the track. Don't let's blow it."

I faced San calmly, but he was close to death, and he knew it. "San. Lindy. *Kantokar?*"

"No!" The chief's face was indignant, stormy. And a good feeling went over me like a wave. He gestured helplessly, trying to make me understand. He had run out of examples. So finally he said, *"Volloon.* Lindy. *Kantokar."*

I pounced. *"Volloon!"* I demanded. *"Ka?"*

The towering slingman's eyes left mine. He stood, tall and bleak, and we could watch decision come into his great bony frame. He waved a long arm in a sweep that included half the looming blue range to the east. *"Volloon!"*

"The mountains?" Pegleg was incredulous.

"Not the mountains," I said. *"In* the mountains. It's something San can't help, but I don't think he likes it much. Check me?"

Pegleg had finally left his jumper, and now he joined us in front of the shelter. I had been so intent I hadn't missed Del, but she had retreated inside. I suppose even she recognized when things had reached the all-man stage.

"Check you," Pegleg said.

I turned to the chief and spoke very slowly, very positively. "San. Pegleg. Roscoe." I pointed as I said each name. Then I swept my finger from us to the range. "Lindy. *Volloon."* I beckoned, then took several strides eastward. Then I looked back.

San was struggling. He was, I realized, fighting a taboo. I smiled, raised a hand. "Roscoe, San, Pegleg, Lindy— friends!" I made it plain. And quite suddenly San's grim blue visage cleared, smoothed, became purposeful and convinced.

"F'iend!" he said simply.

He turned to the shelter, directed a few high-pitched words into it. Then he called, a high, keening flutelike call. The chief was the chief, and he got results.

I didn't see where they came from, but they'd surely had their eyes on us. They had been standing by. We were surrounded in a minute; a dozen extra-tall, blank-faced slingmen, evidently an elite group. Sleek, practically naked, with knives and slings and filled rock bags, each was like a drawn blade.

The chief spoke rapidly. I caught the words "Lindy" and *"Volloon."* He stopped, eyed them coldly. They said nothing; they simply stood, tall, inscrutable, imposing. I guessed that he had put it to them straight, put his authority and his prestige on the line. He waited. Then he uttered a single high syllable. *"Zen?"*

One man answered: *"Zen!"*

That was it.

"The Wildcat's got a load off his back," Pegleg observed. His narrow face was tranquil again, and I knew he was as relieved as I was. "These boys *know* where we're going!"

Chapter 12

The river that flowed by San's village would have been a beautiful thing in normal light. I could picture it in an Earth setting, a wide, gently flowing stream, curving and meandering in sigmoid sweeps across the plains country toward the sea. It would be blue to brown, for there was little sediment in it, but the blue would be contrast, not in conformity as here. Here it was bleak, the color of stainless steel, but still fascinating. Lindy had called it the Blue Danube, and so I thought of it.

I had supposed that the slingmen would set off across country, following trails that they probably had fanning out in all directions from the village. But they didn't. They strode directly down to the river, and to the needle-boats moored along the docks. Pegleg and I had resumed our jumper frames, and we bump-rocked and short-jumped along behind them. From their actions, we might not have been there at all. They ignored us.

Like the trained team that they doubtless were, they launched the dugouts, two men to a boat. The exception was San's craft. It was larger, longer. San himself was bow paddler, and in addition to the steersman, another man sat amidships. The little flotilla knifed out onto the bosom of the river, snaking into single file behind the chief's boat. The long, sinewy bodies of the paddlers gave tremendous leverage to each paddle stroke, and the little boats streaked upstream like water beetles, which with distance they soon resembled.

"Thirteen men," Pegleg said. "I hope that's not unlucky."

"Fifteen men," I amended. "And not unlucky at all!"

I activated my jumper, blasted, and soared a full jump, a

good fifty yards. The country was open; it was easy to pick landing spots. Perfect jumper country. So we began what was to be our pattern all day. We'd blast ahead a few miles, stop at a good vantage point, then stroll and plan until the flashing paddles of our tireless guides showed in the blue distance.

With the foothills, the character of the river changed. It was of course younger, rougher, faster. Our scoutboat cruise over this country—was it only yesterday?—had given us the general picture of this drainage system, and of how and where the Danube came to be. It was the major artery for perhaps two hundred miles, and the smaller streams that wove through our plains country were tributaries.

We stayed closer now, kept the boats in sight. The river narrowed, ran more swiftly, and the hills rose around it. There were sawtoothed rapids, emergent rocks, and then stretches of what in normal light would have been white-water. But apparently the boatmen knew these waters as well as the placid miles below. They picked their route without hesitation, and the classic, tireless swing of the paddlers was beautiful to watch. I had done this, too, in my time; I knew expertise when I saw it.

The river shrank to half the width of the broad stream of the plains. Walls rose alongside it. It came writhing and plummeting down its own gorge as the mountains loomed beyond. I suspected that the boatmen were near the end of the water route.

A small waterfall barred their way upstream, but they flipped the light dugouts out of water, settled them upside-down on their shoulders, and followed a portage trail up over scrubbed rocks and boulder piles to a stretch of smooth water half a mile farther on. They moved more slowly now. And for the first time that I detected, San looked around until he saw us, perched on a prominence overlooking the stream. He raised a long arm and beckoned.

We soared across the gorge, short-hopped our way down the tricky, broken southern wall. When the boatmen came around the next curve, hugging the shore, fighting the current, we were waiting for them at the water's edge.

I've telescoped the day. For Pegleg and me, there had been time for much talk, for observation, for speculation; yet a day as much noteworthy for what we didn't say as for what we said. For we didn't speak of Lindy, nor of the dark-eyed, happy young woman who had been taken with her. We put our thoughts of them in a box, sealed away from our consciousness. Otherwise, I couldn't have gone on.

The slingmen moored their boats in the same neat rank in which they lay along the docks of the blue village. This wasn't their first time. The rocks of the shore were arranged in a pattern. Needle-boats had been tied up here for generations. Here the water trail ended.

I was tired. It was strain, not body fatigue, for the jumpers had brought us easily, could have taken us several times as far. What the slingmen must have felt, I could only guess. For the greater part of a long Hadornian day they had been swinging their paddles, driving on without pause or rest. Their bony faces showed no sign.

We waited for San's lead. He said nothing, but the slingmen, having secured their boats, moved quietly over to a pebbly, cleared stretch of the shore and seated themselves in a rough circle. Somehow they folded their long, skinny legs, wrapped their arms around their knees, and settled into a position of rest that evidently was completely comfortable to them. San joined them, but he sat outside the circle. With a wave of his long arm, he invited us to rest.

"The man knows," Pegleg said. "This is still a long trail, Roscoe." He eyed the relaxed blue giants. "Don't they ever eat?"

"A lovely word," I said, "whether they think so or not. Dinner will have to be buffet, but let's have it."

We had parked our jumpers among the big boulders above the row of boats. We had set our survival packs aside, ready to go. But of course the slingmen's rest made sense. From the packs we had twists of dehydrated meat, dried fruit, pellets which, when mixed with the stream water in a flexible bag, made a pleasing high-vitamin drink. There are other field rations, synthetics, which will provide survival nourishment, but I never use them—I'm old-fashioned.

The blue twilight closed in around us. The slingmen were asleep, each a crumpled knot of arms and legs, like a relaxed spider. From my jumper communicator came gurgles and papery rattles, then a clear voice:

"Dr. Kissinger! Dr. Williams! Relay from Dr. Rasmussen. Can you hear us?"

Only then did I notice the cruising scoutboat, blue light glinting from its featureless metallic skin, swinging toward us from the high range. I ran for my jumper, punched the mike button.

"Kissinger," I said. "We hear and see you. We're on the stream above the waterfall."

"Rasmussen, Roscoe." Johnny's voice took over. "I have your coordinates now. What next?"

"I'm depending on San, Johnny. We're camped now. The slingmen are sleeping. They know where they're going, and they'll take us to Lindy. But what the story is, I don't know. Nothing makes sense."

I suspect he could pick up the desperation creeping into my voice. "You're backed up," he said. "You're only twenty miles from Peters's camp. He has fifteen jumper teams and they're combing all the country west of the escarpment. The Wildcat has followed two trails in, and lost them both against rock walls. That means you're up against something pretty special. It also means that what comes next is up to you. How can we help?"

"Just do what you're doing," I said. "We'll cope. Have scoutboats up there for eyes and ears. We'll keep in touch."

"There's another development," Johnny said. "Dr. Merani's people have been challenged and blocked in the amphitheater. Blue slingmen have come out of the buildings, apparently a large group. They tried to release the man Bud had ironed to the tree, but couldn't handle the magnetic bonds. Bud released him, and they took him inside. Now blue men guard the doors they came through, and the archaeologists have settled down to watch."

I tried to feel the interest that the matchless carvings had stimulated, but it was no go. I couldn't have cared less. Merani and his team were behind their forcefields—they couldn't be hurt—their problems were their own. Only finding and releasing Lindy unharmed had any reality for me.

"The blue man picture is more complex than we thought, Johnny. Somehow, that's why Lindy's gone."

"You'll find her," Rasmussen said. "Out!"

The scoutboat had been swinging in a great lazy circle during the communication. Now it flashed a "see you later" with its lights and drifted on out of sight beyond the next line of hills.

With the last rays of the blue sun highlighting the crags, Pegleg and I restlessly prowled the rubbly, pebbly stretch of shore along the stream. We hadn't worked as the slingmen had, and we felt no need to sleep. We said little. We were talked out. The ideas, the speculations, even the fears that we had, all had been reviewed during the day, during the periods of sitting on eminences, waiting for the boatmen to come into view.

Our setting became gloomier, more sepulchral as the light died. The stream gorge beyond us grew ever deeper. I knew that it actually was one of the larger of the fissures that split and broke up the great plateau north of the amphitheater. Smaller canyons and smaller streams would join it above, a whole drainage network of tributaries. I remembered how the system had looked from the scoutboat.

It required no profound thinking to know that the amphitheater, the incredible carved city, the blue men, the kidnapping, the defection of San (if that's what it was), and our present trail into the wilderness of the plateau, all were parts of a single package. Most of it didn't seem complex, or even particularly unusual. The primitive blue men, taking charge of and using the artifacts of a civilization long extinct—this was believable enough. The fate of the previous race was not in any way evident, but mainly because we hadn't had time to explore. But why the kidnapping? It was not in blue-man character. Why San's strange change of attitude, and then his apparent repudiation of that attitude? Why was he guiding us? For that matter, where? Could or should we trust him? Somehow, I felt easy on this point. The blue men were too overt to dissemble. San's attitude was for real.

I was aware of life in the shadows around me, covert, slinky movements in the boulder piles, small bright eyes peering from the vegetation clinging to the rock walls. Thin high sounds, flutelike calls, disembodied yips, cut through the rippling and gurgling of the water. It sounded busy, but there was nothing ominous in it. I soaked up the atmosphere as a matter of course. A field biologist is a natural receiver, an automatic recorder of such things.

Pegleg, too, was instinctively practicing his profession. His magnifier and small reflector light came into his hands as naturally as my binoculars do to mine. He looked closely at exfoliating boulders, peered at the clean new sections of freshly split and exposed rock wall. He picked up handfuls of the rock fragments we were walking on, which made a long rubble bar as far up the stream as we could see.

"Roscoe!" Pegleg had his light on several small rocks in his hand. A peculiar, almost sheepish smile was on his narrow face. "We do overlook the obvious, don't we?" He kicked a shower of stones from the pebble bar we stood on. "Look at 'em. They all have one thing in common."

I looked.

"Not to me," I said. "I'm no rockhound."

"Tool marks!" Pegleg said in disgust. "I've been walking on them for two hours. Blind as a bat. This is a tailings bar. Not natural fragments at all. Some—in fact, most—are pretty water-worn, but they're chips, just the same."

I picked up a handful. As he said, it was obvious. I nodded slowly. "Figures," I said. "They were fed into the stream as the carving went on. Probably every watercourse coming off the plateau has them. Small fissures may be completely filled. They look natural. That's why we saw nothing from the scoutboat. No piles. No concentrations. They just let the water move them."

Pegleg picked up more chips, ran his light over them, studied them carefully. "One thing," he said. He looked at me thoughtfully. "We are agreed, aren't we, that the carvings are very old. The race that made them, the civilization that they represent—both are gone, we don't know how or where?"

"That's the hypothesis," I agreed. "Merani may know more by now."

He handed me a chip. "When was that cut?"

The tool mark was plain. The fracture was worn almost not at all. It was good granite, but the water and abrasion should at least have mellowed and softened the surfaces of the fragment.

"Many of them are like that," Pegleg said. "That is no remnant from any remote past. A few years, maybe, but it's relatively current. That hasn't seen many winters."

I glanced around me into the blue gloom, as if it suddenly had gained another, unsuspected population. But all I could see was the huddled, crumpled mounds of the sleeping slingmen, and blue moonlight bouncing cold rays off the rippling water.

"If you're saying what I know you're saying," I said. "The carving is still going on."

Pegleg nodded solemnly. "The carving is still going on. And we, my friend, have a whole new problem!"

Chapter 13

The blue moons had traversed the metallic sapphire sky, but the blue sun's rays were still hours away when the slingmen began to stir. Pegleg and I had unrolled our gossamer sleeping sacks and had napped a few hours. We weren't adjusted to the thirty-hour sun cycle, anyway. Normally, the blue men's sleep period would be longer than ours.

We lay in our bags and watched them slowly come to life. They had been lying sprawled, full length on the rough strand of granite chips. Apparently they had shifted position several times during the night. I saw one such change, and they had all done it together. Later we were to learn that there were four sleep positions, assumed always in the same order, and the sprawled prone one was the last before awakening. Just looking at a sleeping slingman you could tell when he went to sleep, where he was in his rest cycle.

The predawn air was chill. Except for the brief breech coverings, the gaunt men were naked. The little flesh on their cadaverous frames was so thinly spread that it couldn't have afforded any protection from the cold, or padding against the sharp points and angles of the rock chips on which they had been sleeping. Yet neither condition seemed to handicap them. How they felt, what they felt, who could say? The bony faces were as expressionless as skulls.

This I'll say: they were wilderness-efficient. They made a morning breakfast camp in less time than I can tell it, and it served every purpose. With a shaped stone and a bit of metal one man struck sparks, trapped them in a wisp of fiber and in minutes had a small reddish flame. Other men brought dead woody vegetation. Two good fires were leaping by the time still other men began to return. Some brought fleshy, poisonous-looking chunks of mushroomlike plant parts. One carried an entire bushy plant covered with thin, triangular blue leaves.

Two men had pushed off in a boat and had gone paddling upstream. They didn't go a hundred yards before they found their game. Then the sternman paddled, the bowman snapped his sling from his arm. The arm whipped, there was a splash, and in another minute they had hauled a dripping body aboard.

It was a villanous-looking thing, an amphibious tetrapod four feet long, its skin shifting blue iridescence and its head not very describable, for the stone had smashed it. But it didn't look edible.

Throughout this disciplined, purposeful activity period San had done nothing at all. He sat at ease on a boulder, his grim visage blank as the rock wall behind him, apparently staring across the stream, but his slanted slits of eyes seemed unfocused, vacant. He ignored everything, including us.

He snapped out of it when the game was brought in. The hunters laid it before him and stepped back respectfully. I didn't see him draw his knife. Somehow it was in his hand, his left hand, and the thin, curved blade was flickering as he did an amazing job on the carcass. In less than a minute it was a crisscrossed pile of limbs and fillets on a flat stone and a small mound of offal on another.

The bluemen wrapped fillets around long, straight branches cut for the purpose, and clustered around the fires. Smells of roasting flesh began to drift past my nose. One man covered a stone with thick slices of the mushroom. San, his reverie behind him, leisurely prepared his own breakfast. And for the first time he looked at us, acknowledged our presence.

"Osco, Pe-leg—eat!" he invited.

We had slid out of our bags, rolled and folded them, tucked them back into our packs. We had our own food, and I was mentally selecting what I'd have. I looked at Pegleg, then turned my eyes back to the unappetizing-looking provender on the stones.

Pegleg didn't hesitate. "Why not?" he said. "We've proved we can eat native stuff. Let's give it a whirl."

So we pitched in. We each roasted a good strip of the meat,

imitating the blue men in taking a blue leaf with each bite. The leaves were for seasoning, bringing out a rather fishy flavor. The fleshy mushroom slices were pungent and crisp. They tasted much better than they looked, which is no great compliment. But it all filled us up, felt comfortable inside, and was presumably nutritious. I felt we had no right to expect more.

The slingmen ate steadily, without haste, and they finished only when the last scrap was gone. Actually, they put away a lot of biomass. The animal had been chunky, and there was plenty of the plant tissue. After the final bite each man went to the stream, lay at full length, and drank for half a minute.

With the same stylized efficiency they threw all organic fragments into the stream, obliterated the fires, and tidied the campsite. When they were finished it would have taken Jubal or the Wildcat to know that fifteen men had camped and eaten there. And I had a warm feeling—a sort of special respect—growing in me for those strange, grotesque giants who observed so concisely the universal rules of the wilderness man: a clean camp and an undisturbed terrain.

Having finished the clean-up, the party was ready to move. But San didn't turn to the boats. As I had suspected, the water trail was ended.

The tall chief seemed hesitant about something; he seemed to be trying to decide how to communicate an idea to us. He looked toward our jumper frames parked among the boulders, then back to us.

Finally he strode away from us for several paces, then beckoned. "Osco, Pe-leg, walk!" he said.

We had taught him that word. He remembered. And he was indicating that the route ahead wouldn't be suitable for jumpers. From here on, we were trail men.

I had anticipated it. Both Pegleg and I wore forcefield belts, which we could activate from a power pack smaller than my hand. Timonium again. It was nothing compared even to the jumper protective field, but it helped. There had been times when just that little repellant field had given me enough of an edge to save my life. Unreinforced, I doubt if it would have stopped a slingman's stone. But it might have blunted the blow.

And a tiny field communicator also occupied a place on my belt. It had a very limited range, but it would reach a scout-boat cruising overhead, a buddy up to a couple of miles away. Better than shouting. Everything's relative.

I indicated to San that we understood, that we were ready. If they could leave their boats, we could leave our jumpers. And the big slingman strode away alone among the boulders. He did not look back. The others stood, relaxed, inscrutable. After half a minute one man left the group and disappeared in the direction the chief had taken. One by one, the blue men followed. They must have been strung out for a mile. The last to leave turned to us, fixed us with unblinking, cold slits of eyes, and beckoned briefly. Then he turned his back and followed the others.

We didn't wait.

"We'd better keep him in sight," Pegleg said. "I suppose they're following a trail of sorts, but we don't have the Wildcat's eyes."

"And what a big, cold, blue, bleak, unhospitable land to be lost in," I agreed. "Still, I can't walk with an eight-foot man. We'll take our regular trail pace. I doubt if San will leave us behind. We're the reasons for the trip."

From the beginning it was a rough trail. It wound around great boulders, across rockslides, in and out of dips and fissures, through small tributary streams. It was the ragged, crumbling, chewed and jagged edge of the plateau, and everything was in giant scale. Stark hills rose around us. The great blue peaks beyond hung over the entire terrain, and between them the blue sun rose.

Yet we could see where the slingmen had gone. Occasionally we got a glimpse of the man ahead of us. Once I saw him standing out against the sky, obviously being conspicuous, waiting for us to come on. We couldn't have gotten lost if we had tried.

It was a long morning. We hadn't been too active recently, and the rugged trail soon took away any bounce we may have had. We plodded along. The bleak landscape encouraged gloom. During the previous day and the camp hours I had been able to focus on the immediate, to keep thoughts of Lindy boxed away, crowded back of my consciousness. But now she came back to me, and with her, desperation and fury. Again and again I had to catch and curb an impulse to become frantic, to rage and scream out my anger and frustration. What was the point of a small handful of men on foot in this vast blue land? Why had this thing happened? Where was Lindy?

Pegleg could sense how I felt. "Take it easy, Roscoe," he said, as we sat for a minute after a steep pull. "Sometimes the slow way is the fast way. We're betting on San. Let's bet all the chips. No reservations—okay?"

"I'm doing it, Pegleg," I said miserably.

His narrow face, with its foxy look, showed both wisdom and sympathy as he grinned. "Not quite," he said. "Occasionally you're ready to blow."

"Sharp man," I admitted.

"I'm not," Pegleg said. "Somehow I'm feeling better every step. It's the very sureness of our blue brothers up ahead there. They *know*. They know what the problems are, too, and I feel that they're committed. San won't let you down. This dragging may set your teeth on edge, but an army and a fleet of scoutboats couldn't do the job we're going to do today. That's simple verity. Keep it in mind."

I held out my hand and my old friend grasped it. "You believe that, Pegleg," I said. "You're not just bucking me up!"

Pegleg stood up and reactivated his plastic knee-joint. "I believe it," he said. "Would I make this trek on an artificial leg just for my health? It doesn't get tired, but after a while it does become a slight nuisance."

You've been ashamed, so you know how I felt then.

"Let's go!" said Pegleg.

A quarter of a mile away, our gaunt blue watchdog moved off the prominence where he'd been standing and disappeared into the rocks.

The great blue wall of the escarpment had been slowly drawing nearer, until it blotted out the mountains beyond. The blue sun lay overhead. I knew that somehow our trail would pierce that wall, that some narrow fissure or hidden canyon was ahead somewhere. That trail wasn't going to get any easier.

I could have told myself that again. We pushed on for another hour and suddenly the cliff loomed up and seemingly over us. The slingmen were waiting, relaxed, inscrutable, sprawled like long blue lizards in a patch of blue sunlight.

San smiled as we came plodding up. It was the first time he had done it on this trip, and I didn't know whether it was encouraging or ominous. As I look back on it, I know he meant it to be friendly. Also, I'm pretty sure he was genuinely amused. We had mysterious powers, we had come out of who knew where; but without our scoutboats, jeeps and jumpers, we were moderately poor travelers on a rocky trail.

San beckoned, strode over to the base of the cliff wall, and looked up. It was a rock face, sheer and raw, and it went up, up, and up. San gestured.

"Osco, Pe-leg"—he had no word, so he simply walked his long fingers up the wall. Then he looked at us quizzically. His meaning was clear.

"Climb?" I'm sure my disbelief was also clear. "Climb that, San? You've got a sense of humor, Long Boy. There's nothing to hold on to."

"You're out of your little blue mind, San," Pegleg put in. "Nobody can climb a rock face without equipment. *You* can't do it!"

"Climb." San picked up the word with satisfaction. "Osco, Pe-leg, climb!" He looked expectant.

"No!" I said. I studied the wall. And, while I'm not the sharpie the Wildcat is, I do have eyes. The rock face before us, and for a strip of maybe ten yards wide, was unusually smooth and bright. It looked polished, almost waxed. It could, I suppose, have gotten that shine by periodic sheets of water flowing down it. But that way, the whole wall would be polished. This was a smoothly buffed band, and it went straight up.

"San climb!"

I dumped the challenge back into the chief's nonexistent blue lap. I suddenly realized that the slingmen *could* climb the wall, that that polished band was the trail, but I wanted to see.

San understood. He gave an almost imperceptible shrug of

his wide bony shoulders. He turned, raised his long arms, plastered himself against the rock face and began to wriggle upward. The tips of his fingers and toes used the smallest checks, fractures, irregularities for clinging points. He was shifting weight from point to point, and his spread-eagled blue body added an infinitesimal bit to the shine of the vertical trail as he seemed to flow upward almost like a worm.

When he was twenty feet or so above our heads, another slingman flattened himself against the wall and began to inch upward with the same unbelievable technique. It was as if they had sucker discs on their fingers and toes, like chameleons and climbing frogs.

In a relatively few minutes there were thirteen spidery figures squirming their way up the polished rock, while Pegleg and I stood, heads back and mouths open. San was so high that his imposing dimensions had seemed to shrink by half. Then he reached what must have been a sizable break in the cliff face, for he drew himself over an edge, swung up his long legs, faced forward and stood looking down at us. One after another the slingmen joined him. They were on a ledge invisible from below.

"Well," Pegleg said, "I guess we're out of it. I make bold to say that we couldn't make that climb if they gave us the planet for a prize."

I had nothing to say.

The slingmen were standing in a strange vulturine row, diminished by height, looking down on us with expressionless faces. I made a gesture of negation. They could see that we couldn't climb the wall.

But perhaps they had guessed it, or had known it all the time. For they fooled us. One man moved easily along the ledge for what might have been a hundred feet or so, then came back with an item we could recognize from below. It was a coil of rope.

San took it from him, shook it free, then tossed a loose end over the ledge and lowered rapidly. I'd have guessed that he was two hundred feet above us, but the rope reached. The end landed neatly at my feet. San's voice came down, thinned by height.

"Osco, climb!"

If there had been a way to back out, I'd have done it. But there wasn't, and a man has pride. I picked up the rope end, looked at Pegleg, and shrugged.

"Here goes nothing," I said. "Watch me, and do just the opposite."

I tied the end around my waist with a good bowline, passed the rope over my shoulder and through my legs in a sort of reverse rappel rig. I put one foot against the wall and gave San a wave. He seemed to understand. He tightened the rope, then he and the man beside him began to pull me up hand over hand.

It wasn't so bad. They pulled steadily. I kept my legs stiff, my boots flat against the rock, and literally walked up the wall. Before I could believe it, long blue hands grasped me. I was safe on the ledge.

I suppose "safe" is the word I want. The wide places on that ledge may have been eighteen inches; there were plenty that were ten inches narrower. I made myself thin against the wall and tried not to admire the view. A few minutes later, Pegleg was flattened beside me.

"What a way to have adventures to tell your grandchildren," he said.

It was a trite remark, but it hit me strangely. "If this adventure doesn't go right I won't have any grandchildren," I said grimly, and suddenly the height was meaningless.

Pegleg got it. He slapped me on the shoulder. And I knew that the height meant less to him, too.

San wasted no time, but he took no chances with us either. He knew we were out of our areas of competence. We started along the ledge and there were blue men behind and between us as well as ahead. I felt almost confident, but not for long.

The ledge held up well for maybe a hundred yards, then came to an end. And upward I could see again the polished surface of the vertical trail. San spread himself against the wall and began once more to wriggle skyward. And one after another, the slingmen followed. But not all. One remained on either side of Pegleg, and two also watched me. As I said, San was taking no chances with us.

The climb wasn't as far as the first had been, but it was terrifying enough. And to stand immobile on that narrow shelf of rock during the slow ascent of the men above was as nerve-racking as anything I have ever done. When that rope end finally came slipping down it was beautiful.

I tied my bowline, double-checked it, and gave San the wave once more. After I got my feet against the wall and they began to pull, I knew I could do it. I was too busy even to sweat. But it was not a thing I'll ever learn to love.

Pegleg followed, and then our blue guards came slithering up on their own. San didn't move until the last man was on the ledge.

This ledge couldn't give the other one much, but I fancied it was wider. After we had inched our way along it for a couple of hundred feet or so, I knew it was. And then the fissure which I had expected to show at the base of the escarpment finally appeared. The ledge clung to the side of it. The trail became two, then three feet wide. We could stride along normally, if that's possible while threading the raw face of a cliff hundreds of feet above the first outcrop that would catch your falling body, and with a thousand feet of blue wall above you.

The fissure widened, until the wall opposite us was about fifty feet away. It knifed deeply into the plateau, a dark, jagged split that seemed to go on and on. But our ledge spread and developed an overhang above. We turned onto a smoothly worn platform that would have held fifty men. There was no doubt what had formed it—or rather, what hadn't formed it. This was no freak result of erosion; it was artificial—a vaulting, wide-mouthed cave gouged deep into the granite.

The blue men threw themselves down on the polished floor and lay sprawled, completely relaxed. I had been so concerned with my own problems that I hadn't even thought about the terrific physical feat each of those lank, inscrutable giants had performed. It was superhuman. But they were tired, and they lay for a while like dead men.

I stretched out, myself. I was not only weary; I was weak from reaction and strain. Pegleg grinned at me wanly as he sat slumped against the chiseled wall. "Always where the action is—that's us, Roscoe. But you know, I think I'm getting a little old for this sort of thing."

"I was always a little old for this sort of thing," I mumbled. "I never figured myself for a sissy, but these boys are something else. I wonder how they get down again? Jump?"

Pegleg shuddered.

"I'd believe anything." He looked around the cave. "Is this a way-station, a sort of rest stop, would you say?"

"Could be. The road may get a little rough, farther on."

Pegleg slumped back and closed his eyes. I suppose he couldn't face it. Without Lindy before me every minute, I don't believe I could have. I lay prone on the smooth stone, blanked out my mind and slept.

I woke from a hard toe in my ribs. San stood over me. He smiled down from his great height, and I know it wasn't perfunctory. He was amused. "Osco, walk!"

I sat up, then got to my feet with a groan. "Walk, he says! With all the good hiking terrain around here, why not? You mean climb, San!"

"Walk," the giant said, and waved a hand.

Chapter 14

It hadn't been there before, but it was there now. At the back of the cave a wide tunnel mouth gave access to a blue corridor, with ample headroom for the tall slingmen who already stood inside it, and dimly lit by some blue light source I couldn't see.

"I don't care where it goes," Pegleg said. "It's beautiful!"

I shrugged into my pack, making sure my guns were swinging the way I like them to swing. I strode over to the front of the cave, stood at the edge of the access ledge, looked up and down the dark, raw canyon, and out the narrow slit to the spreading, sunlit blue land to the west. I suppose I had been in more unusual situations, but I couldn't at the moment remember when.

I turned back to San. "Lead on, friend! If you've got rougher stuff coming up, let's have it while we can still take it!"

The blue giant shrugged and moved into the passageway. The men stood aside to let him go by. The slingman nearest the corridor entrance pulled a ponderous metal ring in the wall and a slab of stone slid smoothly across the opening and fitted itself with a click! Outside, the chiseled cavern was probably simply that, with no sign of the tunnel that now curved away into the depths of the plateau.

Pegleg jumped to examine the ring with his small reflector flash. The slingmen waited patiently.

"An alloy, Roscoe. Heavy, hard, and very finely textured. Etched with a carefully worked symbol. Whoever did this represents an advanced technology."

"The door mechanism tells us that," I said dryly. "That thing weighs a number of tons."

Pegleg grinned a little sheepishly. ''So it does. I think of one thing at a time.''

San beckoned, then strode off down the corridor. Four slingmen stayed close at his heels, and the remainder grouped behind Pegleg and me. The deployment was obvious and significant. They walked no faster than we found comfortable and kept the group compact. They didn't look concerned, but that was meaningless, for their faces never expressed any emotion at all anyway.

The tunnel illumination was dim, a thin blue radiance that seemed to come from six-inch bars inset at infrequent intervals in the wall at about blue-man shoulder height. Footing was good. We strode along at regular trail pace, and ahead we could see the corridor dwindling into distance.

We traveled almost silently. The bare feet of the slingmen whispered on the smooth stone. Pegleg and I have developed the quiet tread of wilderness trail-men. Occasionally an item of equipment would rattle or clink, but on the whole it would have been hard to hear us coming.

Someone did, though. Or something.

The thin, high, keening cry rippled and wailed down the corridor, and San brought his party to a halt. He spoke briefly to the blue men, then turned to us. Firmly he indicated that we were to stay in the middle of the group.

''Volloon!'' he said simply.

I chilled, but I felt the adrenalin flow, too. Here the *Volloon* had taken Lindy! I fingered my laser gun grips. If Lindy wasn't all right, a great many other people or things were not going to be all right either.

''Take it easy, Roscoe,'' Pegleg warned. ''Let San call 'em. We don't have the rulebook handy. We don't even know what the game is.''

San led on again. His stride was as confident as before, and when the keening wail came once more, he didn't pause. He did something more disconcerting. He answered it.

The high flutelike call that issued from his thin lips was, in a sense, familiar. At least, I remembered when I had heard it last. Out in the grainfield, where San and his slingmen had first pitted their slings against our forcefields. And I felt cold again. Lindy was in all my memories.

Out in the grain the blue man's cry had been one of astonishment. Here it sounded defiant. I divined that the wail of the *Volloon* was a warning, and that San wasn't interested. He strode on grimly. The corridor seemed to have no end.

The next warning wasn't sound, but it was pretty basic. The lights went out. For a moment the light bar nearest me seemed to fluoresce, a dim glow that soon faded. And the blackness was absolute.

I could feel the slingmen all around me. But San kept moving. He must have expected this. It was as dark as the inside of a black cow, but somehow the slingmen were keeping in touch. I suspected at least a latent telepathic empathy. Apparently they knew the corridor, knew what it could provide in the way of menace. We moved on, guided by a sort of epidermal radar that became more acute as we accepted the darkness.

"Electric system, Roscoe." Pegleg's disembodied voice was at my shoulder. "Those lights are activated by a current."

"Possible," I agreed. "But I wouldn't be too surprised at something a lot more sophisticated."

"Doesn't faze the slingmen," Pegleg said. "They don't have TV in their huts, but this is old stuff to them."

"Apparently. There are a lot of pieces missing from this puzzle, Pegleg. The lights-out gambit is nothing but a harrassment, if I read San's reaction correctly. He doesn't seem to expect anything drastic."

"If you can tell, you're good," Pegleg said. "Wonder how they'd react to a magnaflash?"

"Save it," I advised. "We know we can light up the place if we have to. Let's just keep it for a surprise."

We got the surprise, though. I'd hardly pronounced the word when I plowed into the slingman ahead of me. There were muted rustling as we packed together. San had halted. We stood, soundless in the utter blackness, and I felt the slingmen separate and spread out. A faint musky odor drifted from the corridor ahead; then we could hear rasping scraping sounds.

"Attar!" San's voice was deep and urgent. It also

sounded indignant, as though somebody wasn't playing the game by those rules Pegleg had mentioned.

The slingmen formed a phalanx of interlocked arms around us, and we all moved backward a few paces. I sensed, rather than heard, the swish of a sling—and a solid, melon-like thud followed. Again the swish, and this time there was a crack far ahead in the corridor. Someone, probably San, was using a sling, and he had one hit and one miss. The odor welled around us now. The rustling and scraping up front was louder and closer, as though whatever made it was scrambling or struggling.

"Magnaflash!" Pegleg said. "You be the gunman."

The brilliant white light flooded the tunnel. I pushed past the immobilized slingmen, my laser gun out and on wide beam. I didn't want to fuse the rock around us.

San stood five yards ahead of us, a third stone already in his sling. Beyond him, and not far beyond him, either, a long writhing something flung scaly coils against the corridor walls, twisted and plunged and struggled. The musky smell was sickening and strong.

The chief's horoscope must have been featuring a whole flock of favorable signs, for his first stone had been a bull's-eye. Or a snake's-eye. The thing was a pretty fair analog of an Earth snake, but far larger than even the biggest python. Its alligatorlike head was a smashed mess. San's first stone must have hit it as it swung sideways in the back-and-forth motion that seemed to characterize creatures on this planet. This was a guess, of course. I'd not seen one of these things before.

San adjusted quickly to Pegleg's flash. He darted forward, his curved knife in his left hand. Two slingmen followed him, knives glittering. They pounced on the great coils with their horny feet, holding down the front end of the creature while San's knife probed and ripped under the scales behind the mutilated head. In a moment the head sagged, although the yards of heavy body behind it kept up an uncoordinated lashing. This soon changed to a series of shudders, and then the thing lay still.

San looked coldly at the thick, dark blue blood on his knife, and at the long heavy cylinder of the monster's body. In the smashed head, imposing rows of sharp teeth showed.

"Attar!" San said. *"Volloon attar!"* His disgust was evident.

"That's a *Volloon?"* Pegleg was incredulous.

"I think not," I said. "That's an *attar*. It was released by the *Volloon*. San thinks it's dirty pool."

The chief nodded.

"Volloon attar!" He switched his cold gaze to the magnaflash, which Pegleg directed downward, but which illuminated the area around us perfectly and without shadows. He pointed a long finger. *"Ka?"*

As tense and upset as I was, I had to grin. Pegleg laughed aloud. "Always the student, San!" he chuckled. He gestured with the flash. "Light," he said, and repeated the word; "light."

San saw no humor in the situation. He turned his broad back, beckoned with the dripping knife. "Pe-leg, light, come!" he said.

He strode away, avoiding the coils of the dead *attar*. Pegleg followed, lighting the way, and I came third, a laser gun free in my hand. Behind us the tall slingmen formed a mighty backup guard.

There seemed to be no breaks in the tunnel walls, but probably that didn't mean much. I remembered how neatly the terminal door had fitted. I guessed that this corridor could be entered at many places, and that even a careful search might not always reveal the doors. The whole plateau was probably a maze, a network of tunnels, rooms, caverns. I let my imagination go. The possibilities were endless.

As I rethink that trek into the plateau, that long jaunt along the tunnel of the *Volloon,* I can't recall any particular doubt, any fear that we wouldn't be able to handle any emergency that showed itself. It was spooky, playing tag with something we couldn't see. But I didn't think the *Volloon* were trying to do us in. They were making motions, warning us; they didn't follow through.

We hadn't gone ten minutes beyond the big snake before the tunnel lights came on again. They were barely detectable in the white flood of the flash. Pegleg switched it off, our eyes adjusted, and we strode along in the blue gloom.

And then the corridor ended.

That's right, it ended. The end wall showed the same chisel marks as the sidewalls. It looked natural, but it wasn't, of course. We had just come around a bend in the tunnel, so we hadn't seen it happen. It may have dropped or slid into place long before we got there.

San looked chagrined. Pegleg switched on his magnaflash again, and it was easy to see the small crack around the door or barrier or whatever it was.

"Clever little people," Pegleg said. "I've got a feeling they could have done this before."

"San's running a bluff," I agreed. "They're coming closer and closer to calling it."

We watched San, who was checking every inch of the crack around the barrier with painstaking care.

"I'd feel easier in my mind," Pegleg said, "if I knew what I mean when I say 'they.' Since that *attar,* I begin to feel that this chunk of granite we're worming through is considerably more populated than it looks."

"Well put," I applauded. "I think San's stymied. They've deactivated the door control."

The chief straightened from his task. He looked beyond me and his cold eyes widened with anger. I heard a soft rumble and turned in time to see the granite wall slide into place a few yards behind the last slingman. We were cut off.

"They could have done that, too, apparently," I said. "We haven't been listening, so now they're going to play rough."

Our walled-in section of tunnel was perhaps fifty or sixty feet long. Call the tunnel height ten feet, its width twelve or fourteen. That was the size of the room the *Volloon* had created and tucked us into, neatly and with no fuss.

"If this isn't a main traffic artery," Pegleg said dryly, "they can keep us here forever. Hope they remember to pipe in a little air. The high oxygen is one of the things I like about good old Hadorn."

"What they pipe in doesn't have to be air," I said. "They probably can make us plumb uncomfortable, if they take a notion."

I was interested in San's reaction. He didn't seem worried about air or *attars* or anything of the sort. By now I had watched him enough to read him, at least a little. And San was indignant, royally angry. You felt that the lion's tail was being pulled by the jackal. He pretty obviously hadn't believed that this would happen to him.

He came up with the solution, though, all by himself. He strode over to me and tapped the butt of one of my laser guns with his long fingers. Then he pointed to the barrier ahead. "Osco, gun!" he growled, his voice as deep as I'd ever heard it.

I admit to mild astonishment. What he wanted me to do was plain. He apparently believed that the gun could punch a hole in the wall and, like the chief he was, he was ordering it done. He couldn't know that what he believed was modest compared to what was possible.

I set the gun for a cutting ray, thumbed the stud, and a thin, almost invisible beam sheared down one side of the rock barrier. I was lucky. Not only did I cut through the door slab, but I happened to hit the lock mechanism. Released, the slab retracted smoothly into the corridor wall. Our way stretched ahead, unobstructed.

There was regal triumph on San's blue face. He beckoned and we moved on in the blue light.

The *Volloon* must have been discouraged. They tried nothing more. The dim blue lights never flickered, and we strode on at trail pace for perhaps another half hour. But this is no account of an endless march. The corridor had an end.

It flared suddenly into a high-vaulted cavern, and the feel of spaciousness after the tunnel's closeness made me take a deep breath. Pegleg's sigh must have been caused by the same thing.

"Now," he said, "we're getting somewhere!"

"Where?" I asked.

"Don't push your luck," Pegleg grinned. "I've told you all I know!"

But San knew. And since the bit with the tunnel doors, he took no chances. He barked a sharp order, and the tall slingmen formed a wide ring around us, every sling swinging free, and a rock in every pouch. We moved slowly out into the cavern, Pegleg and I looking about curiously. We've been in so many unlikely spots that we can pretty well take anything in stride. And this was simply a big cave, obviously chipped out by the same techniques that had made the tunnel.

Illumination wasn't good, but we could see. And what we saw made no sense whatever. The place was full of boats! Well, not really, but there must have been three or four dozen of them, neatly set up in rows on wooden racks. They were needle-boats, differing in no way that I could see from the ones that had brought the blue men up the Danube from the village.

"Now I see how we'll get out," Pegleg said. "Simple. We just paddle down a waterfall!"

"You're just full of them today, aren't you?"

I get a mite impatient with Pegleg sometimes. The tighter the situation, the more puckish he gets. And with this new, more open space, I was brought back sharply to the realization of why we were here. There were tunnels and caverns and probably subterranean rivers, a vast network under hundreds of miles of granite. Men—or beings even more advanced than men—had been chiseling away under this plateau for eons. Here we had to search out the creatures called the *Volloon*. And here, somewhere here, they were holding Lindy! Suddenly I was in no mood for bright sayings.

I flipped out a laser gun with my right hand, pushed past the circle of slingmen and joined San, who had moved over and was examining the boats. My patience had given out. "San!" I said urgently. I patted the gun. "Lindy? *Volloon! Ka?*"

As irritated as I had become, I was conscious of a wish that San had learned a few verbs along with the words he knew. It was almost as exasperating not to be able to ask questions as it was not to be able to *do* something.

The big fellow understood. He stood looking down on me almost tranquilly, his blue slits of eyes faintly sympathetic. Perhaps he was reflecting the pride he felt in his own woman, and he knew how I felt. His thin lips compressed. He raised his bony shoulders in the faintest hint of a shrug, a gesture that was completely *human*.

"Osco, wait!"

Now there was a word I didn't even know he knew. And it fitted this situation like a glove. What else could I do? I could run amok and shoot up the place, but that wouldn't bake any apple pies. So I simply stared at the calm giant, gritted my teeth, and shoved the gun hard back into its holster.

"Okay, big man, you're the boss! But let's get with it. We're close now. I feel it. So rattle the bones! Let's go!"

I was so right. A section of the cavern wall turned slowly, as though on hinges. A wide portal yawned, and beyond it we could see the ripple and glint of flowing water. But that wasn't all.

A blue man strode slowly through the opening. I say blue, but he just barely made it. He was fungus-pale, the dim blue lights of the cavern causing him to appear even more cadaver-like. He was as tall as San, and incredibly thin. Or what we could see of him was thin. For, unlike any blue man we had ever seen before, he wore a robe.

Our slingmen deployed in a wide half-circle, swinging their loaded slings gently. San paced toward the cave dweller, but his sling remained wrapped on his right forearm. Pegleg moved over to where I stood, my hands on my guns. It was a big display for what seemed to be a rather fragile old man. But we took our cue from San. And he was tense. We could feel it.

He halted perhaps three yards from the robed man. Silently the two stared at each other, each in his way both arrogant and regal. Then San swiveled his long head and looked briefly at us.

"*Volloon!*" he said.

Chapter 15

Well, you could have used my head for a football. I don't know what I expected, but I do know that this would have been away down on the list. A monster with many heads, slavering jaws, breathing fire and blue smoke like a Hadornian Fafnir—that I would have accepted without much surprise. The very name *Volloon* had evil in it to my thinking. But of course that was simply a buildup in my mind, with nothing tangible to hang it on. We only knew what the *Volloon* presumably had done. This gangling skeleton with the cold slit eyes actually made the most sense.

"San!" The robed man's voice was high and brittle.

"Ben!" San's own high voice was arrogant, but there was a reluctant respect in it, almost a deference.

The *Volloon* spoke rapidly, half a dozen high phrases. San replied briefly, positively. They stared at each other in silence again, cold blue gazes locked.

"A slight difference of opinion, maybe?" Pegleg's sour voice sounded almost happy. He loves it when things get to the point.

"If I could understand their palaver," I said grimly, "I'd clear things up in a hurry. They'd see judge, jury, and executioner all wrapped up in one hairy skin."

"Take it easy, Roscoe." It had become Pegleg's theme song. "Let San do it. For some impossible reason the *Volloon* is holding a high hand, including the queen of trumps. This isn't just a caper. It's rooted in the whole pattern of the lives of these people. Notice San had a little trouble not pulling his foot and touching his forelock? He's shattering custom, speaking up to old Bony there."

I'd noticed that. I thanked my blue stars that San was a proud and an arrogant man, who would, I felt sure, break any taboo rather than back down or lose face. He was committed. If something had to give, it wasn't going to be San.

The *Volloon*'s thin voice came on in measured cadences. He was speaking slowly, positively, and with finality. Near the end of his harangue I caught a word I had heard before. It was *"kantokar."*

"No!" San's deep explosion was in English. He followed it with a rush of Hadornian, his voice going higher and higher. Then he turned and gestured toward us. There was violence in his movement and naked anger on his bony face. But the *Volloon,* not having had the advantages of association with us, showed no expression whatever. He looked us over, spoke a single crisp phrase, then turned and stalked back through the portal. Two robed paddlers steadied a boat in the flowing millrace beyond, the *Volloon* stepped in, and the boat shot away downstream.

My gun was out, but San stepped in front of me. He held both hands palms out. He struggled for words. "San— Osco—Pe-leg—get Lindy!"

He had picked up another verb!

He waved to the slingmen. The rocks vanished magically into the pouches, slings wrapped themselves on right forearms, and the blue giants turned with swift efficiency to the boats.

San, Pegleg, and I occupied the middle passenger seat in three-man boats. The others were two-man jobs. The *Volloon* had gone downstream, but our boatmen bent their lean backs and fought the current. The channel was narrow, so the water was fairly swift. We made reasonable progress, though, and San seemed to know where we were going. We were simply in a slightly larger tunnel with a stream in it. The chiseled walls, the dim lighting bars, the very texture of the granite, all were familiar by now. I felt as if I had been underground for weeks.

But not too many minutes later, a carved and chiseled platform—a dock, of sorts—showed up. It was on the opposite side of the stream, but our boats swung alongside, our boatmen grasped worn granite outcrops, and we followed San through a portal which slid open when he pulled a ring.

The cavern we found ourselves in was far greater than the

last, and its contents infinitely more puzzling. There were more boats on racks, and extra racks that the blue men used to cradle our boats neatly. I'd have expected them.

What I didn't expect were the rows and rows of shelves and racks, each holding a miscellaneous assortment of what I can only describe as junk. It was like a huge packrat's nest, and it took me a minute to realize the significance of the stuff collected there. It was all alien. By that I mean that none of it, as far as we knew, could have been made or used by the blue men of Hadorn. Sheets of metal, springs, rods, all kinds of odds and ends. The blue men had knives, but no other metal that we were aware of. I had thought fleetingly that the knife steel seemed to be of fine quality.

There were other things. Piles of fiberlike stuffs, sheets and rolls of strange-looking plastics, rows of stacked coils of pliant cords and ropes. Only then did it occur to me to wonder at the sophisticated look and feel of the ropes San and his boys had used to drag us up the cliff. Here, obviously, was where they had come from.

But most of this stuff was unused. This was a storeroom, a sort of collection center. We wandered slowly along the rows of racks, looking, touching. The blue men deployed around us, and I could vaguely sense San's impatience.

"What do you think, Pegleg?"

"Two categories," Pegleg said promptly. "Unused supplies and salvage. Most of the metal is pickup. And all of it so old there's no guessing who made it—or where."

"Not on Hadorn," I said.

"You're getting those facts you wanted," Pegleg admitted. "Not on Hadorn. But nothing to link it to Earth, either."

"There will be," I predicted. "We're into things now. If we weren't so weary, we'd probably have ideas. Maybe the blue boys can go on forever, but I've about had it."

Pegleg's limp had been showing for a while, and it was no put-on, I knew. He sat wearily on a convenient flat roll of cordage. "Twenty miles of mean trail, up two cliffs, six or eight miles of tunnel, assorted disembodied hecklings, one *attar,* one *Volloon* (or was it three?), one subterranean canoe trip. You know, that's more than a standard union day."

"And no time-and-a-half," I agreed. "We've got to make

haste slowly. Some shut-eye is indicated. Those stacks of canvaslike stuff look comfortable.''

I tried one. The material was soft and flexible.

"Like baby's blanket," I reported.

I stretched out. Pegleg promptly followed suit. We got no argument from San. The blue men slumped down wherever they were, arms wrapped spiderlike around legs in the number-one sleep position. There were two exceptions. One tall slingman positioned himself between us and the stream portal, while San himself settled to watch the other side. I don't remember going to sleep. I don't remember anything more.

Chapter 16

I awakened to the tantalizing smell of warm roasted meat. I thought it was the end of a nice dream, so I lay for a moment with my eyes still closed, savoring it. Pegleg and I had nipped bits from our survival packs during the long march, but we'd had no solid food for a long Hadornian day, and, presumably, night as well. I was famished. The good smell persisted, so I slowly opened my eyes.

That seemed to open my ears as well. The blue men were all up and busy. Their bare feet whispered on the stone floor, and they were actually talking to each other in soft, high tones. Each man was working on a big slab of meat, held directly in long blue fingers, and torn at by strong blue teeth.

San was sitting, meat in hand, watching us with that quizzical, almost amused look that was his commentary on our poor traveling competence. I rolled off my stack of bedding and sat up with a groan.

"Osco, Pe-leg—eat!" San said. And he actually grinned.

I shook my head violently. It didn't come off, so I knew I was okay. I stood, stretched until my joints snapped and my empty belly caved. "Okay, you blue reincarnation of Satan," I growled. "Where is it?"

It was almost in front of me, a big wooden salver piled high with roasted slabs of meat. I drew my knife, impaled one, and sank my teeth into it. It was luscious.

"Blasted barbarians!" It was Pegleg's groan behind me as he checked himself over to see if he'd last another day. Apparently he got a favorable report. He rolled to his feet, limped over to the meat supply, and helped himself.

I suppose I have had better balanced breakfasts. Any nutritionist would have been disconcerted at the amount of flesh I tucked away, supplemented and modified by nothing, at all. Just meat. I didn't even wonder what kind of creature had provided it—I ate and was glad to get it.

But as good as I am before a plate of food, I couldn't complete with the slingmen. There were three big platters of the meat and they ate, calmly and steadily, until the last scrap was gone. Then they turned to a huge ceramic jar, as big as a large barrel. A stack of wooden bowls stood by it. Each man took a bowl and they dipped and drank, until I thought they'd never stop. I recalled how they had drunk from the stream, at that other breakfast so far behind us that it was dim in my memory.

Finally they quit, and Pegleg and I had a sip. It was just clear fresh water, cool and good.

"Essence of blue thumbs," Pegleg mumbled, but he drank his fill, as did I.

We were ready to move before I had sorted things out in my mind. Once sorted, they fitted and made sense. Things like how the blue men could come up with a cooked meal deep in these caverns of what might reasonably be called enemy country. It wasn't complex when I thought about it.

Basically, it wasn't enemy country. San was evidently completely familiar with the setup. In some fashion all the blue men were connected with it. The *Volloon* was—or were—blue. They knew each other well. All these things were evident when I sorted them out.

Probably blue-man customs pertained here. Somewhere within easy march I could envision a communal kitchen pretty much like the one that served San's village. The chief had simply sent several men to bring back what we needed. Paradoxical? No doubt. But I'd have given odds that that was the answer. And, as we later proved, it was.

The slingmen tidied up in short order. San spoke to them briefly, then turned to us. "Osco, Pe-leg, come!" he said.

"I feel so futile," Pegleg complained, as he swung up his pack. "I'm losing my personality! That big goon has been ordering us around for two days."

"He doesn't mean it like it sounds," I soothed him. "He's handicapped. If he knew more words, he'd be more considerate of your standing in the community, your place in the social stratigraphy."

"I doubt it," Pegleg grinned. "When a man is born to command, don't get in his way! It would take a lot to convince San that he's not the boss."

I swung up my own pack. "Right now, he is. He's also the only hope we have of finding Lindy and Barbara and getting them out of here. Only he and his Merry Men know what the problem is."

We followed San across the cavern. The usual ring in the wall activated a smoothly sliding slab of stone. We moved into another tunnel, and the gaunt slingmen deployed around us like blue shadows, their faces as blank as the tunnel walls.

"Merry Men!" snorted Pegleg.

I hardly had time to start to dread another long tunnel hike when we came into another cavern. Like the last, it was full of stuff: metal, ropes, cordage, and rows of metal-bound chests. My curiosity hurt, but the thought of Lindy was pushing forward now, crowding out everything else. We were close. Somewhere in this incredible maze under the plateau, the *Volloon* were holding two Earth women. And one of them was my wife.

We were in a chain of caverns linked by short sections of tunnels that were wider and vaulted higher than the one that came from the escarpment face. We followed the blue men through half a dozen, each of which seemed part storeroom and part museum. I promised myself a good look at all this when we had fulfilled our mission and things were happy again. Pegleg strode along beside me, face to the front, but I knew that later he'd be able to detail every feature of the rock from which these caverns had been chipped, bit by bit.

We could feel life all around us. I was sure we were being watched every step we took. How, I had no idea, but the blue men knew. They were ignoring it, and we had no choice but to follow suit.

But we couldn't ignore the seventh cavern. It was all museum. Pegleg's pose of indifference dropped from him like a sloughed skin when he saw the long lines of neatly mounted skeletons.

"The good old Smithsonian!" he said, and stopped to stare.

"Hardly," I said. "It never saw the day it was as good as this."

"You can say that again!" Pegleg stood before a compact skeletal mount that even my eyes could recognize as piglike. His narrow face was a study.

"So I could," I said, "but you heard me the first time. You're seeing more than I am, Pegleg. Tell!"

"Oreodont!" Pegleg didn't sound like he really believed it. "Miocene! Earth Miocene!" He stood tall, and his eyes flicked along the rows of skeletons. Pegleg had had no superior in Earth historical geology before the *Stardust* first left the Solar System. He wasn't talking at random. He was seeing unbelievable things. "These are Earth skeletons, Roscoe. You can push coincidence only so far." He shook his head. "Earth skeletons, but not recent. Things like these haven't walked our green hills and prairies for millions of years. These are Miocene forms. As near as I can tell, every blinkety-blank one of them." He looked quizzically back at me and grinned. "Now it's your turn," he said.

I don't know why I thought of it. I've read a lot, but obscure geological quibbles aren't high on the list. Still, something flashed in my mind.

"Pegleg," I said, "remember the Ramsgate Paradox?"

Pegleg considered me for a moment in silence, as though I were one of the specimens.

"Yeah," he breathed softly. "Roscoe, you've got possibilities. Sometimes you almost convince me that you're an educated man."

"Don't strain yourself," I said. "Just cogitate. This is all so farfetched that anything that fits seems reasonable. Suppose old Ramsgate had something? How do we know how far his hypothetical culture developed?"

You're lost, I know. Here's what we were talking about.

Some fifty years ago a so-so geologist named Elias Ramsgate opened up a dig in a Brazilian canyon back on Mother Earth, and began finding stuff so different and so out of place that nobody believed it belonged there. After his first paper, he was enthusiastically labeled a fake by all his friends and contemporaries. But as more and more of those same friends

saw the ever-increasing amounts of evidence, criticism gave
way to confusion. The Ramsgate digs became famous. Ol-
duvai Gorge couldn't compare. But nobody concurred with
Ramsgate's conclusions.

For in obviously Miocene deposits Ramsgate found
strange metal artifacts, exquisite remnants of ceramic con-
tainers, areas of fused glass and, most stable of all, indica-
tions of building foundations, structures of incredible mag-
nitude. But plant materials, animal remains, the strata that
enclosed them—all were Miocene. Further, nothing remained to indicate that a civilization had died out or deterior-
ated here. How could there have been? When those strata had
been laid down, man was still millions of years in the future.

It was Ramsgate's hypothesis that became the Ramsgate
Paradox. For Ramsgate had concluded that there had been a
civilization here, a civilization before the rise of man. And he
went farther. He stated that that civilization had not degener-
ated, had not faded away. His explanation: it had migrated.

That accounted for the fact that nothing had been preserved
intact. Ramsgate postulated that all materials not carried
away had largely been destroyed by the beings that had lived
and grown and developed there. Only unexplainable fragments were left.

There's a lot more of it, but you get the idea. Nowhere else
on the planet Earth had Ransgate artifacts been found. So the
migration could have been only in one direction. Outward.
Toward the stars.

Why? Ramsgate had suggestions. How? Ramsgate offered ideas. But it was all too speculative. Ramsgate was
famous mostly as an irresponsible explainer of fragments.
Still, there was so much material, so many fragments, that he
had left his science with the uneasiness of problems still
unsolved.

As it happened, Pegleg had examined those digs, had
looked over the unlikely artifacts recovered, had been as
puzzled as geologist-archaeologists conventionally were by
the worked metals, the pottery fragments, the apparent evidences of advanced technologies. I remembered that now, as
Pegleg said slowly, "That's what's been nagging me, Ros-

coe. I knew I'd seen stuff like those piles of metal strips, those curious-looking alloys in this spelunker's paradise we've been going through. May I be expelled in disgrace from the geologists' union if those aren't Ramsgate metals! I remember some of the stampings. I don't forget stuff like that.''

I knew he didn't. I'd take his word over the *Encyclopedia Galactica,* if he insisted on a point.

I had another idea. "San!" I called, and raised a finger.

The tall chief, who had been waiting with commendable patience while we palavered, took three strides and loomed above us both.

"Lend me your knife," I said. I pantomimed, touching my own knife, pointing to his, then holding out my hand, palm up. "Knife," I repeated.

He knew the word. He trusted me, I think, but he wasn't about to be given any orders. He drew his knife with a single fluid movement of his bony left hand, but held out his right to me, also palm up.

"Osco, knife!" he said. Pegleg chuckled.

I drew my knife and placed it on the long blue palm. Only then did he reverse his grip and hold out his weapon to me. I took it, and grinned at him.

"He understood me. But nobody makes this boy lose face."

Pegleg and I put our heads together over the slender, curved, glistening blade.

"Same type of material? This is finer than Swedish steel. Tempering of this quality would be beyond slingman capacity, wouldn't it?"

"Same," Pegleg agreed. "Roscoe, when we get this can of sardines opened, we're going to find all sorts of things inside." He straightened. "Give the man back his toad-sticker. I'm going to give these bones a quickie."

San and I reexchanged knives, while Pegleg wandered slowly along the rows of skeletons.

"Fantastic!" he muttered.

I caught up with him, and he continued his soliloquy, partly to himself, partly to me.

"Could have been a colonizing ship—or ships—bringing domestic animals as well as pets. Many of these are herbivores. Probably would have made good eating."

"Well-preserved bones to be so old, and out in the open like this," I said.

"There's some ultraviolet in this glow. We'd do well not to look directly at those light rods. I doubt if decay organisms could live here. Lindy could tell us in short order." He realized that that was the wrong thing to say, so he made it worse. "We'll bring her by, before we leave. She'll be interested." I couldn't tell whether it was a phony expression of faith, or if he really believed and meant it.

We worked through the cave. San finally grew impatient.

"Osco, Pe-leg, come!"

"Just hold your hosses, San, old buddy. The best way to make haste is slowly. I'm gathering clues, like the late Mr. Holmes." Push Pegleg, and he promptly drags his feet, no matter what the situation.

So we all had to wait while he worked his way along the cavern wall, checking skeleton after skeleton, murmuring notes into his little recorder.

And suddenly he just wasn't there.

Chapter 17

It was easily explained. Naturally we hadn't watched every minute while Pegleg puttered and procrastinated. And that's what he was doing, partly. If you have a talent for orneriness, you have to keep it honed with practice. He hadn't liked being pushed and directed by the blue chief. He was interested in the specimens, of course, but he was also saving face. In the peculiar way that Pegleg looks at things, he was reestablishing his own self-respect.

So the blue men had relaxed their vigilance a trifle as we waited, and apparently a little was enough. Pegleg had been standing by the wall, his back to it. A door must have opened, long blue arms have snaked through, and Pegleg was snatched from the cavern before he could utter a sound. The faint click that I'm sure I heard must have been the door settling back into place.

San glided softly to the spot where he had last seen Pegleg. At the same time the slingmen closed around me, a protective wall of gaunt blue bodies. A sling swung free from each long right arm, a stone in place. Deliberately the chief studied the wall. Then he turned away.

"Osco, come!" he said. "Find Lindy, Pe-leg!"

My laser gun was in my hand. I had burned through one door. There was no reason why I couldn't do it again. But San vetoed it.

"Gun, no!" he decreed. "Osco come!"

Well, he had to know. At least, he was better fitted to decide than I was. And for some time now the anger and indignation that had driven me before had been slowly ebbing. I knew I had to take things as they came.

I was even conscious of a faint amusement. I could envision Pegleg, in durance vile and mad as a wet hen. Somehow,

133

life-and-limb danger still didn't seem a part of the picture. I
didn't believe that the *Volloon* was out to kill. It—or they—
just wanted to be left alone with their caves and artifacts. We
were butting in where we were not wanted. They'd go to all
reasonable lengths to get that across before the situation
became deadly. San's attitude had told me that all along. And
now his mien was more one of anger than of any other kind of
concern. Pegleg's life wasn't in danger, my intuition told me.
But I won't say that I didn't wish I had Ursula handy to
confirm it.

We left the cavern of the skeletons. San paced ahead. All
around me loomed my bodyguards, gaunt forms between me
and every wall, cold, inscrutable slit eyes flicking from every
skull face. The loss of Pegleg had offended them, I knew.
They didn't plan to lose me. And in a way the snatching of
Pegleg was actually bad news for the *Volloon*. It had been
poor judgment. Nobody on this cold blue planet could tweak
San's long nose and get away with it.

The tall chief knew where he was going now, and he made
short work of it. I was glad of the long rest and the plentiful
feed, for I surely needed them. The slingmen must have
figured that they had babied me long enough. Try to match
strides with eight-foot giants for an hour—it's an experience.

The tunnel we followed narrowed until it was not much
wider than a single slingman's wide shoulders. Twice it
branched, and each time San chose without hesitation. The
intervals lengthened between the inset light bars, but the pale
blue glow was enough to travel by. Finally the tall leader
slackened his pace. I shortened my stride gratefully. San
seemed to be looking for something. He inspected the tunnel
wall carefully, running his fingers over the chipped stone. He
directed a high-pitched phrase behind him, and one of his
gaunt henchmen pushed past me. Together they rechecked
the wall. Then San beckoned to me with a long forefinger.

"Osco, gun!"

It was an order, and for a moment I felt the same stubborn
resentment Pegleg had shown. Then I grinned. Here I was
just a soldier in the ranks. I drew a gun, adjusted it. "Okay,
Big Boy, where'll you have it?"

The big fellow with San looked at me with a knowing gleam in his slit eyes, almost as if he understood. And it was his bony thumb that drew a line down the wall to show me where to cut.

"Gun!" San said.

I pressed the stud. The thin ray of almost irresistible energy rearranged the molecules of the stone along that line. I could see bright light through the slit. But nothing moved. San's big lieutenant, if that's what he was, drew another line down the wall six feet away and motioned. I looked at San.

"Osco, gun!" the chief commanded.

That one did it. As my gun muzzle neared the floor of the tunnel the whole slab of wall slumped downward and then fell away. Beyond a wide corridor vaulted high, brilliant with yellow light.

San leaped through the opening, his loaded sling swinging gently at the end of his mighty right arm. His lieutenant followed. Several of the others brushed past me. The now-familiar circle of blue bodies enclosed me, every man ready for action.

I wondered if the slightly comic aspect of the situation occurred to them. They were protecting me as though I were a helpless lamb or a downy chick; yet they knew that I had at my fingertips forces that could destroy anything the *Volloon* might loose against us—or, for that matter, the *Volloon* themselves. Twice they had called on me to shear through walls even they could not have broken. I was sure that some of them had been with San when I crisped up the birds.

Still, their concern for me at least had a point. Pegleg, too, had had a gun swinging at his hip. And Pegleg was gone.

The corridor we had broken into was wide and high, but the remarkable thing to me now was the light. Big glowing yellow globes thirty feet above our heads made the whole area bright as Earth day, and completely changed the appearance of my gaunt blue companions. Oh, they were still blue. The yellow light showed them to be several shades, ranging from San's almost metallic blue hide to the smoky gray appearance of his grim lieutenant.

The light was not quite the balanced blend that you

associate with a yellow sun, but it made the colors of the spectrum possible. I realized that my new appearance must have startled and interested my guards. The circle around me spread, and I could see that each pair of long slit eyes was studying me with covert curiosity.

They were justified, I admit. Since the blue light of Hadorn obscured or distorted most colors, I hadn't given much thought to how I might look to the general public when I had dressed for this foray. I had worn what was suitable for rough country; what was tough, what was warm. Blending color schemes had been no part of my concern. So when the yellow light revealed my scarlet thermal jacket, the warm blue-and-white striped knitted cap that protected my head, my green thermal breeches and high, flexible black boots, they were entitled to stare.

They couldn't criticize, though. The sole garment of a slingman was a breechclout around his bony hips. The bright light revealed that each was a different color. Whether it was deliberate, whether they even knew it or not, I couldn't then say. It made no difference so long as they showed as varying shades of gray.

"Look and enjoy yourselves, boys," I invited. "I may be a bit conspicuous in this light, but I'm just your same old buddy."

I grinned openly. San smiled, but briefly, and I was sure I detected a smirk on a couple of other faces, including that of the tall lieutenant. He was usually near me, and whenever I spoke he seemed to listen with unusual intentness. But the corridor was serious business to San. He spoke a few high words; the slingmen deployed and spread so that the loaded slings would not be hampered. He expected to be challenged. I divined that the other tunnels and caverns were familiar to the blue men. This corridor was a part of a different world. It was more truly of the realm of the *Volloon*.

San gave a sharp, high order. We all paced forward slowly, maintaining the spread pattern, no man obscuring the sling path of his neighbors. Anything ahead of us, if the going got critical, could expect flight after flight of thirteen well-directed stones. I shook the grips of my lasers, loosening them in their holsters, just in case the opposition turned out to be a little more sophisticated. I regarded myself as the second line of defense.

The slingmen couldn't know the restriction under which I operated; that I would deliberately take the life of an aware creature only to save my own—or that of a *Stardust* mate. I was hoping against hope that the *Volloon* would parley, that they would listen to San.

We hadn't long to wait.

I couldn't tell where the voice came from, but it was familiar, high-pitched and indignant; a typical blue-man voice. It harangued us for half a minute.

San's response was curt and brief. There was neither awe nor respect in it now. He spoke as a chief.

The angry voice rang out again. Seemingly the hidden *Volloon* was getting set for a lecture, but San cut it short. I understood two words.

"Lindy! Pe-leg!" The blue giant's voice deepened with the names. The sentence that followed was gibberish to me, of course, but there was no mistaking the tone. The chief was demanding.

"Man, oh man, that's lettin' 'em know! I'll tell the world!"

It was the kind of silly speech Pegleg often affected. It was almost Pegleg's voice. But it had a parrotlike quality, as though the speaker were performing by rote. It actually took me a minute or so to locate the source, but it had to be nearby, for it was scarcely more than a whisper.

The blue man closest was San's cadaverous lieutenant. He had moved up until he was almost behind me, and as I turned and stared up into his skull-like face, one slit eye closed in a deliberate wink. He gave me a minute to think about it. Everyone else's attention was riveted on the unseen *Volloon*.

"You spoke English?"

The big fellow's thin lips barely moved. "I got some words. I can carry a tune in a jug. You dig me?"

It made no sense at all. "I understand," I admitted. "But where did you get the words? You never heard speech like ours before we came."

"Natch. Got 'em from Pegleg. You. Put 'em together. No problem."

To my astonished ears that seemed just slightly oversimplified. But my curiosity had to wait. San had given a crisp order, and our deployed squad of blank-faced giants, loaded slings swinging gently, moved off down the corridor. There had been no agreement, and San was challenging the *Volloon*.

Chapter 18

It may have been a half hour later—a most remarkable half hour later. If the cavern of the skeletons had recalled the collections of the Smithsonian, the series of vaulted rooms into which the side corridor led us could easily have matched wonders with the Louvre or the Rijksmuseum. San slowed his pace. The blue giants stared at the incredible works of art on the walls of space after space, their slit eyes unreadable. I could feel their astonishment, yet I also had the feeling that they had known that these things were here.

It wasn't just the color, and this wasn't simply art for art's sake. The magnificently pictured panoramas, the meticulously depicted buildings and gardens—and the portraits! especially the portraits—these were more than art. They were history; the history of the race that had grown on Earth and migrated to the stars. These told a part of the story of the people of the Ramsgate Paradox.

There were paintings twice as tall as a slingman and stretching for a dozen paces along the cavern walls. There were smaller ones, all sizes and shapes, by the hundreds, many of them ornately framed and all carefully hung and displayed. Some seemed to be on canvas of a sort, but more were on the resistant plasticlike substance on which our picture of the cathedral was drawn; the picture given to us by San on his visit, and now hanging in our bedroom.

And there were tapestries woven of fibers unknown to me, brilliant with color and with strange, yet familiar scenes. Cloths of obviously metal strands were suspended in heavy metal frames, and on these, too, were paintings, drawings, pictures produced by techniques I had never experienced before.

I wasn't overwhelmed. I was beginning to get an inkling of

what all this meant, but I needed to talk, to express what I thought, to bounce my ideas off somebody. That was a major function Pegleg and I served for each other. And Lindy! Never was my thinking clearer than when I discussed things with Lindy. My anger began to grow again. It was tempered, though, by the thought that the beings that had maintained all these artifacts over what surely must have been millennia would cause no real harm to other beings who came from the stars. These were my thoughts, and I needed to put them into words.

"San says *move*."

The low monotone at my shoulder came as both another surprise and a reminder. I looked up at the gaunt slingman's expressionless face.

"You tell San," I said slowly, "to soak his head. I'm looking."

"Like wow," the big fellow said. "No water." His slit eyes regarded me steadily. "You mean different."

"I mean different. Does San know you can talk to me?"

"He knows"—the lieutenant sorted through his vocabulary—"he knows that I do not lose sounds. Once I hear, they stay. You dig?"

"You're saying, I think, that you have total recall. And San knows that that's your talent, your gift. Right?"

The slingman nodded solemnly. "One right thing. I got more. San knows."

That was a little garbled, but I thought I knew what he meant.

"You also have a name," I said. "It would help."

"Ron."

"Okay, Ron, we've got to talk. Will San mind?"

"San will like. I talk to you, talk to San. San talk to you, by me. Right? Right!"

"Or to put it a little less primitively, you will act as interpreter. I think you can do better than that last speech. Don't pretend with me. You're good!"

Ron's cold eyes narrowed until the pupils could not be seen. I thought he would surely smile, but his bony face stayed as still as the chiseled wall. "I can do better," he said carefully. "Whenever you speak, I learn. I have many words now. Most meanings are clear. You dig?"

"I understand." I nodded, but mentally I was shaking my head. This gaunt blue giant had to have more than the ability to remember sounds. Not just anybody can learn a complex language in a few days of eavesdropping. This boy was sharp. Most of our speech had context completely unknown to him, yet evidently he had worked it out.

I didn't fight it. No matter how he had managed to learn, I intended to use what luck provided. He could tell me about all this—and the *Volloon*.

"Where are we," I demanded, "and where are we going? What does San have in mind?"

"San keeps his thoughts," Ron said. "We have never seen these treasures before. We have never been in these—" he hesitated for a word.

"Caverns," I supplied.

"Caverns," he said. "These caverns are new to us. But the *Volloon* are here. They keep the treasures until the Sky People return. They have done it through all the ages since the world turned blue."

The big lieutenant's voice deepened, and he spoke with a rolling fluency that improved with each sentence. He had put the words together in his thinking. Now all he needed was practice.

So there was a history, there was a legend of Sky People who came and went away again, and of a time when the world was not blue.

"Who are the *Volloon?* Who gave them the job of guarding the treasures? What makes them special?"

"They say," Ron said slowly, "that the Sky People put the task in their hands, and that all men should help with the cutting of the stone and the making of tunnels, and the carrying away of small pieces. They say that the Sky People spoke that they be given food—meat and grain and leaves— so that they could care for the treasures."

"You mean that you, whom we have called the Blue People, have done all this tunneling? *You* feed the *Volloon?*"

"All men do their share. There are many villages. All give help."

"Pretty nice for the *Volloon,* I'd say. And what do you on the outside get out of it?"

"The *Volloon* say that in these ways we help to preserve the treasures. When the Sky People return, they will be pleased."

The big slingman's face was immobile as always, but a different tone had crept into his voice when he quoted the *Volloon*.

"That's the *Volloon*'s story. What do *you* say?"

"I say that it's a lot of bunk!" Ron's voice was deep and scornful.

It was Pegleg's favorite expression.

I had grown so interested in the talk that I'd forgotten for the moment where I was. San reminded me. He had circled back and stood towering over me, his slitted eyes flicking from me to the noncommittal face of his giant lieutenant.

"Osco, Ron, talk?" San was still no linguist, but he had learned to put the question mark into his voice.

"We talk," I agreed. "Tell him, friend."

Ron favored his chief with two high, brief sentences. San replied, even more briefly, but I could tell that he wasn't displeased. He would rather have done the communicating himself, but, like me, he would take what chance provided. He gave me a last look with those cold eyes, then barked a sharp command as he strode away. The slingmen deployed as they had before.

"San says talk later! Move now!"

There were more caverns of the pictures, and I didn't doubt that they constituted the etched, drawn, and painted art of a nation—perhaps of a whole race. It was too much to take in, too much to grasp. The dome lights made the colors almost true. After the long hours in semigloom or in the blue Hadornian light of day, it was restful just to stroll past the landscapes, the mountains, waterfalls and oceans, with Earth clouds above them and strangely familiar animals and birds. By now I knew why I recognized them. They were of Earth, but Miocene Earth.

Then came whole rooms of portraits. I strolled more

slowly here. San did not object. He himself was looking with attention at the fine-featured, carefully depicted faces of men, women, children; people not of his world; the Sky People. And I'm sure he saw what anyone could see; that they could have been my people as well.

"That's it!" I spoke aloud. The eyes of every man of my blue guard flicked in my direction momentarily. Ron ranged alongside me.

"Idea?"

"A big one," I said, "and I'll bet I'm slow with it. You've already thought of it—and so have the *Volloon.*"

Ron waited.

"Those are the Sky People. They're supposed to have gone away long ago. They left the skeletons in the cave, the ropes and the metals, all the junk we've seen. They left these pictures."

"They left more," the slingman said. "You ain't seen nothing yet."

"I've seen this. Those people look like us. They could have come in our ship, in the *Stardust.* For all you know, we could be a Sky People group, come back to check on our property."

I've said that Ron was sharp. Now he showed something else: a grim sense of humor. His death's-head face began to break up; his slit eyes crinkled; his thin-lipped mouth slowly widened into a genuine grin. Then he chuckled. "The *Volloon* are afraid. They never thought Sky People would come back. They ain't going to give these things up."

"Yeah," I said. "They'd be out of a job. They'd have to go to work. Make their own living. After all these centuries, what a horrible prospect!"

"Hard lines," said Ron.

Each time he came up with another Pegleg expression, I marveled again at this gaunt blue primitive who wasn't a primitive at all. I'm used to genius—it abounds on the *Stardust.* But the uncanny recall and the instant comprehension that let Ron speak meaningful English—I hadn't seen its like before.

"Osco, Ron, see!"

San didn't have Ron's ability, but he was trying. He stood

before a rather small, simple portrait, richly framed in ornate gold. He waved a bony hand, then stepped aside to let me look. And I admit to a little chill for a moment as I studied the painting. I saw what San saw.

It wasn't Lindy, but it could have been. The resemblance was almost too great for the coincidence that it had to be. They were Lindy's green eyes that looked from that familiar, beautifully planed face. The faintly smiling lips, barely parted, with just a hint of white teeth between, were Lindy's lips. No one would know better than I. And the upswept mass of red curls, piled regally high, was uncannily like Lindy's. Shapely, perfect shoulders and arms, magnificent bosom . . . every detail was right. But the total impression was not quite familiar. The personality was that of a stranger. It was as if a perfect makeup job had just missed. So I knew it was coincidence—but I could see what the *Volloon* would think.

"Like wow!" Ron breathed. "Hot dog! Good try, but no cigar!"

"I couldn't have said it better myself. You remember people as well as you do words. You saw her only in passing, but you can tell that that's not quite right."

"Saw her more than you think. She taught Mel to say 'friend.' I looked at her close. Good gal."

"Closer, apparently, than I looked at you. You're Mel's man? That visit, you fellows all looked alike to us. Sorry."

"No sweat," Ron said. "We do look alike." For the second time in half an hour, he grinned. "Pegleg spoke to my kids. Patted them on their heads. They liked that. Mel liked it. *I* liked it. Good guy!"

The big fellow was telling me more than the words said. He really knew what 'friend' meant, and he was saying that I had one. Further, that Lindy and Pegleg were real people to him, and that he liked them, and that this wasn't just a job. I haven't too often had a feeling like I had then.

"Is 'thank you' in your list of words, big man?"

"I dig it," Ron said gravely.

"Well, have a helping of it from me to you, and pass it on to San. Whatever happens, I'm grateful to every man in the group. You tell 'em for me."

"Will do, you bet. Just one thing is going to happen. We

get Lindy and Pegleg. That picture tells why they wanted her. I'm not sure what they're thinking, but she's safe. Keep your pecker up!''

"Learning English from Pegleg has its hazards," I said, "but I'll always be thankful that he never stops talking!''

When Ron said that I hadn't seen nothing yet, he was telling the simple truth. I think he hadn't seen them either, those other things, those artifacts of the Sky People whom we both knew had existed; I because of the Ramsgate Paradox, he because of the artifacts that he could see and feel, and because of the legend that was part of his life. Whatever their origin, they were not of Hadorn.

We were in the storage complex now, chains of lofty caverns that extended for miles. These were rooms that the blue workers from outside ordinarily never saw, though the spaces had been chiseled out by their ancestors. I think perhaps chiefs from the settlements and villages had been favored. However he may have learned, San seemed to know his way through them.

He had a plan, too, and one that the *Volloon* could not counter without active resistance. And by now I suspected that they didn't dare risk that. At any rate, we weren't challenged again. We saw no living thing. Each great room was brightly lighted, filled with carefully arranged and completely incredible artifacts, and as utterly deserted as the gardens in the amphitheater of the carvings. And for the same reasons.

We were watched. There was no evidence of it, and we didn't know how it was done, but I felt sure that every move we made was seen by more than one pair of eyes, and coldly analyzed. The *Volloon* had not had a problem like this before. Probably they realized that it was of their own making. They may have regretted it. But they were committed, and they were following through, at least for a while.

Their idea, it seemed, was simple. We could wander and search as we chose. We'd see the treasures of the Sky People, but all men knew that they were there. The mazes of caverns and corridors were so large and so complex that it would be impossible to find anything they wanted to hide. They would move the prisoners, keep them out of our way. It was passive and effective.

"San's got something in mind," I said to my big blue shadow. "We're not just random tourists, I hope."

Ron considered for a moment, probably grappling with 'tourist.'

"Tourist, sightseer. One who looks at things out of curiosity. That's not why we're here."

"Thank you for nothing," the slingman said. "I dig you. Takes time, but I can put it together. San knows we can't find those who have been taken."

"So?"

"San will take something in return. He keeps his thoughts. I do not know what he will take, but the *Volloon* will not want it to go."

"Bright idea. But suppose they decide to keep us all. We could just vanish, couldn't we?"

Ron's cold eyes narrowed, as they always did when he had unpleasant thoughts. "Too great a danger for the *Volloon*. They would not want the food to stop. They would not want many times our number of slingmen pouring through the corridors and caverns."

"You think that would happen? Your people think that the *Volloon* are the chosen of the Sky People. Would they dare? How would they even know?"

"It is known that we are here. And there is another reason. Del. San's woman. She came from the *Volloon*. She knows."

Leaving me to ponder these tidbits, Ron moved away. We may not have been here for sightseeing, but by now I could tell that the slingmen weren't wasting their opportunities. While they were alert for any trickery, they gave the marvelous contents of the storage caverns the same intent scrutiny they always applied to everything. When they returned to their village by the cold Blue Danube, they'd have a tale to tell. And I'd have bet that they would be able to list the things they saw with a completeness I couldn't begin to match.

They could have trouble with terminology, though. The great cavern we were passing through set up an entirely new train of thought for me. For the slingmen it must have been pure mystery. Carefully mounted on racks, or in some cases assembled in complicated arrangements on the stone floor, were control panels of an elaborateness that would have confused Cap'n Jules's technicians. I'm no mechanics expert, and I probably got little more from them than the slingmen. That wasn't the point; the point was that there were dozens of them, all apparently in perfect order.

I could imagine salvage from crashed ships, all kinds of broken and deteriorating odds and ends, picked up and preserved by whoever found them. But nothing like this. For me an impression was growing of something far more significant.

I began to suppose. Suppose that the Sky People had never left Hadorn. Suppose that that whole flotilla of starships— twenty? thirty? more?—were still here, dissected, spread out piecemeal through hundreds of caverns. When they had left Earth, they had destroyed everything they left behind. Would they have done less here?

Then what had become of them? Were they still here? Were the *Volloon* simply trained watchdogs, directed by superior intelligences secluded still more deeply in this incredible maze of caverns, tunnels and corridors? Were they playing god at the direction of beings that they thought were really gods.

There were more questions than answers. And there were contradictions. For my conviction had never wavered that the blue men were human; Earth-human. And it was obvious that the *Volloon* were blue men too. San's wife was of the *Volloon*. I didn't understand that, but I didn't doubt it. And aside from that, the three *Volloon* that I had seen differed in no essential from the inhabitants of the blue villages around the great grainfield.

Chapter 19

For some minutes I had been aware of a soft hum, and an occasional light crackle and rattle. I should have recognized it at once under other circumstances, but here, deep under the plateau, I knew that communication with my coworkers from the *Stardust* was impossible. I had forgotten that there would be one exception. Pegleg! The hum came from my own little belt communicator. It was on hush setting, and something had turned it on. I pressed the transmit button and whispered.

"Roscoe! Good man! Use your glottis mike. They're probably watching us both."

Pegleg's voice was clean and clear, so I knew that there wasn't too much distance or too much rock between us.

"I'm amazed that they haven't taken your stuff," I said. "Are you all right?"

"Inconvenienced and annoyed," Pegleg said grimly, "but otherwise okay. They just took my laser. They knew what it was, so look alert. They may have figured out how to use it."

"I think they won't dare—I hope. Meanwhile, we'll try to find you. Any ideas?"

"I'll stay at this power level, and speak every five minutes. Your volume should pick up with decreasing distance. There may be all kinds of interference, but it's our only bet. Can you get it across to San?"

"You forget," I said in a hurt tone. "I'm a linguist. We'll talk it over. You're as good as out right now. As a friend of mine advised recently, keep your pecker up! Out!"

Pegleg's chuckle came plainly. He didn't know what I was referring to, naturally, but that was one of his favorite admonitions. I had no time to tell him of the phenomenon of Ron.

Even the talking we had done was probably conspicuous.

At my end it certainly was. San's slant eyes quickly saw me talking to nothing. Ron drifted up behind me like a ghost.

"Pegleg," I told him. "We have a small device that talks from a distance. You understand?"

"I dig. Where is he? If we go near him, the *Volloon* will know."

"But will they know that we know? Tell San that I can guide us to Pegleg. We'll just have to take that risk."

The blue chief loomed over me. Ron spoke to him at length, the high tones almost whispered. Ron evidently had a considerable respect for the ability of the *Volloon* to know what was going on. San listened impassively. Then abruptly, as usual, he gave his order.

"Osco go!"

The chief had spoken. But I think it still galled him that Ron could converse and he couldn't. So he added, "San, Ron, all—come!" His death's-head face was almost as triumphant as when Lindy had taught him to smile.

"Lead on," he was saying. "We'll follow you!"

The cavern we were in was the size of an auditorium, wide and high-vaulted. The assorted displayed and stored machinery would cause considerable interference, and I suspected that the lighting system might affect our signals as well. To say that I could guide to Pegleg was the optimistic view—I suppose I should have said that I could try.

I waved the blue men back while I paced back and forth and up and down the length of the big room, listening intently for any change, any intensification of Pegleg's signal. It was tricky. Even without all the metal about, the distance was too short to give me much variation. But finally I made up my mind, beckoned to the slingmen, then stood aside for San to go before me through the exit I indicated. Ron crowded close behind me. I noticed that his long knife glittered in his bony left hand.

The corridor we came into was a T, and I picked a direction at random. Before long, the weakening signal showed that I had chosen wrongly, so I had the embarrassment of retracing my steps. But I didn't explain. The slingmen were accepting my guidance, and how I did it was none of their affair. They simply followed.

The other direction was pay dirt, though. Pegleg's signal grew steadily stronger. I thumbed my transmit button and risked a verbal check.

"We're on our way. Signal's picking up. Are you tied or shackled, or just locked in? Any watchers or guards? Do you read me?"

Pegleg's low voice fairly jumped at me. "Loud and clear. You must be close. I'm in a good-sized room. Only one door that I know of. I may be watched, but I don't know how. I can't even see how they aerate the place. Air's okay, though."

I guessed that there were limits to the *Volloon*'s imagination. Even though we were deep into the maze of treasure caverns now, they wouldn't suspect that we could locate Pegleg through thick rock walls. So although we would pass nearby, they wouldn't move him. His prison was on this corridor. I felt sure of that.

The communicator hum rose to a crisp purr. There was a barely discernible door outlined in the corridor wall. It would slide, I assumed, like all the doors we had seen in this world of rock. I slipped my laser from its holster and adjusted it.

"Which side's the lock?" I asked Ron.

He understood, and pointed with a long forefinger.

I spoke to Pegleg. "I think we've arrived. Stand away from the door and get your magnaflash ready. The one thing they might do is turn out the lights."

"Ready," my speaker said. "Let 'er rip!"

I drew the thin blue beam down the faint seam in the rock. There was a soft click as it ripped through the metal of the bolt. The door recessed and slid smoothly into the wall. San leaped through the opening. Pegleg stood grinning in the middle of the bare room, his right hand gripping the magnaflash he didn't need after all. Several of the slingmen surged around him, while others deployed in the corridor.

"You meet people everywhere," Pegleg said. "Sorry for the inconvenience, Roscoe. I was stupid. Anybody can have a bad day, you know."

"I never do," I said gravely, "but then, I'm unusual."

I held out my hand, and the handclasp said something quite different. With Pegleg back for support and backup, I felt like I could function again.

"Put her there, pal," I said.

In a way, the handshake was a poor idea. San never stopped learning, and this was a thing he could do. He loomed over Pegleg, and put out his mighty blue hand.

"Pal," he said.

And then each slingman had to go by, put out a great hand, and say "Pal!"

"I feel like a one-man receiving line," Pegleg muttered, but he shook each big hand heartily. There was no doubt that he was glad of the chance.

Ron came by last of all. "Put her there, pal!" he said, and it could have been my voice. Because I was watching, I could see the gleam in his cold slits of eyes, the faint twitch of his cadaverous face. Ron was not only an authentic genius, he had a sense of humor.

Pegleg looked bewildered for a moment. "Are you a ventriloquist?" he said to me.

Ron's frozen features thawed and he grinned. "Play it back once," he requested. "I can guess meaning, but I haven't heard it before."

"This is Ron," I explained. "You didn't know it, but he has learned English from you. As a result, some of it is a little informal, but he can talk like a congressman. I know it's not very believable, but accept it as a fact, just the same."

Pegleg looked thoughtfully at the strange blue giant. "Yeah," he said. "You're the one with the crooked nose. No offense, but I had to have something to tell one of you from another. Come to think of it, you've been at my elbow ever since we started this junket."

"You talk a lot," Ron said. "I wanted all the words I could get. When Roscoe wasn't near, you talked to us, or even to yourself. I needed you."

That was all understatement. I've implied here and there that Pegleg is verbose. I've recorded some of his conversations when they were pertinent. But to have set them all down would have filled a volume of the *Congressional Record*— and not have been much more significant. Pegleg thinks behind a wall of words, ninety percent of them in the no-man's-land between trivia and utter rubbish. And as near as I could tell, that long blue sponge had soaked up every syllable.

"Ever have a mirror held in front of your face, Roscoe?" Pegleg now inquired. "One showing all your bad habits? I hope you realize," he said to Ron, "that I didn't know you could follow that stuff I sometimes said to all of you. I was just blowing off steam."

"Right on," Ron said, with a wave of a bony hand. "We won't fight about it. We said worse about you."

We might have stood and palavered like a bunch of old women, but San called us to order. There was crisp impatience in his tone. "Osco, Pe-leg, Ron! Go! Get Lindy!"

Part of San's annoyance was probably due to the fact that he couldn't understand the talk. Nobody was about to leave the chief out of things. But his cold voice, uncharacteristically deep, brought us back to now—and rightly so.

The slingmen spread out in the wide bright corridor. San directed a brief, high sentence at Ron, then led off with purpose. He knew where he was going.

That we had been able to find and rescue Pegleg was simply a fluke, and we knew it. Lindy and Barbara were something else altogether. The *Volloon* had taken Pegleg largely for harassment, or so I believed. But what their thinking was in the kidnapping of the women was becoming more and more obscure, especially since we had seen the portrait.

I filled Pegleg in on what he'd missed as we strode along. "Thinking it over," I said, "it's a good thing you got snatched. That hurt San's feelings. Without it he may not have been willing to use strong-arm stuff to break into the treasure caverns. He had me burn through the wall."

" 'They also serve though only used for bait!' " Pegleg grinned wryly. "I know. Bad pun. We're moving along pretty spryly now. Any idea why?"

"Ron says that San is going to take something that the *Volloon* will value more than our women," I remembered. "Then he'll make a trade."

"Like what, for instance?"

"He didn't say. Didn't know. 'San keeps his thoughts' is the way he put it. Which reminds me: you have met the *Volloon* socially. What are they like?"

"Rough," said Pegleg. "Just like our boys here are rough. For that's all I saw. They're simply blue men, complete to the knife, but with no slings. There were three bully boys to handle me, and one long Slim Jim in a kimono to tell them what to do. They hustled me through half a dozen corridors, finally out into the light, and dumped me where you found me. Took my laser on direct order from the foreman, but didn't bother with anything else. They didn't even offer me a dish of tea. Fortunately, they left me my own."

"That's it!" I said. "Now I know why I feel weak. I'm hungry. We've been going for nearly an Earth day without food."

"The slingmen have eaten only twice since we've been on the trail," Pegleg mused, "and then after they have slept. Must be custom."

"Each time they ate a heck of a lot," I remembered. "And drank like camels. It's a handy habit, but I don't have it. If San doesn't stop before long, I'm going to call a dinner break."

"I had nothing else to do in my little private suite, so I filled up." Pegleg patted his stomach. "I was so hacked, though, that I was lucky not to get a belly-ache. Now what?"

San had known where we were going, and we had arrived. The corridor ended. A great ornate door blocked it, a recessed stone door like all the others we had seen, but the width of the corridor, and easily four or five feet taller than the towering slingmen. And it was more than a door—it was a work of art.

The style was familiar. The same flawless sculpture that comprised the buildings in the amphitheater was manifest here. The fine granite must have been murder to carve, but the result was worth it. The entire face of the door was a picture in bas-relief, its closer and more conspicuous features boldly depicted and extended, objects in the distance etched almost as delicately as frost on a leaf. And the picture told a story. All the viewer needed was a knowledge of the history of the Sky People, and I'm sure it would have been a familiar story. That we didn't have, so we had to use our imaginations. As I think back, I believe we made some good guesses.

A man—an Earthman—was the closest figure. He stood with his back to us, obviously looking out and down on the scene that lay in the distance. There rocket ships stood in ordered rows, each with a gantry beside it, and a wide, glinting pad on which it rested. They reminded me of the specimens in museums of the old fire-tails of the late twentieth century, but there were conspicuous differences. These were not cylinders; they were flattened, though they sat on end, and each had wide, wing-like projections on either side, rather like star-seeking bat rays. For that was what they were—starships. This was the transportation of the Sky People, the people of the Ramsgate Paradox.

San was a sensitive man. He stood like a big blue carving himself, grim and inscrutable, while we looked. He had seen it before, I thought; perhaps had even had it explained to him. But I doubted that the story the *Volloon* would tell was the real explanation. Or had they had passed to them a history as authentic as the artifacts they guarded? There was no way to know.

Beside me, Pegleg heaved an incredulous sigh. "Unbelievable," he said. "Roscoe, I've been there."

"Would you be trying to tell me that that's the Ramsgate Gorge? And you a geologist? Further, there's no gorge; it's a plain. There are low hills in the distance."

"You stick to ecology," Pegleg advised. "That's the Miocene, remember? It became the Ramsgate Gorge. What disastrophism and erosion, what uplift and wear-away went on, I don't have in mind. But we do know that the site shown here on this door was still identifiable when Ramsgate made his discovery."

"I'm glad we do," I said. "It's the first I've heard of it. Maybe you'd better tell me how we know. I'll sleep better, not having to puzzle about it."

"Count the ships," Pegleg directed. "Thirty-two, right? Three zigzag rows. That's neither a random number nor just an artistic pattern. That's the way it was.

"Ramsgate measured and diagrammed that field. It had been tipped and gouged and covered, but he worked it out. Since the Miocene people had either loaded their effects onto the ships, or for all practical purposes destroyed them, the researcher had only bits and pieces to work with. But thirty-two blast pits, thirty-two fused silicon bowls, arranged in three zigzag rows; these told him how his people had gone. Unfortunately, they didn't seem reasonable to anyone else. What Ramsgate regarded as his strongest data, everyone else thought should be his admission ticket to the loony bin. People didn't have spaceships in the Miocene. There were no people in the Miocene. The human race did not evolve until fifteen or twenty million years later."

Pegleg looked at me quizzically. "Choose. Which side are you on? I saw those pits. And there before you is a carving of the ships that made them. Looking at the ships is a man, an Earthman."

"I can't count his chromosomes," I said. "He—and they—could have come from anywhere."

Pegleg studied the bas-relief and nodded slowly. "There is that," he agreed. "Earth could have just been a way station. The Sky People may not have evolved on Earth. But I think they did. I think this was the only exodus they ever made. I think that when they landed here, this world was not blue. And I think they died here."

"At least," I said, "you think. At another and less rushed time, I'll listen with interest to where the blue people came from, and how it happened that Earth independently evolved two human races."

"I'm glad you put it off," Pegleg admitted. "There may be a couple of details I haven't worked out yet. Let's battle the *Volloon,* free Lindy, and then we can take time for introspection."

San was waiting patiently. When he saw that we had finished examining the carving, he pulled the ornate ring that activated the door mechanism. The great slab dropped smoothly into its groove and slid into the wall. Shoulder to shoulder, San and Ron strode through the opening. We followed, and the slingmen crowded on all sides of us, a bright knife glinting in each huge left hand.

We had found the *Volloon*.

Or, perhaps, this was where they had chosen to meet us. They must have realized that we could not be stopped, could not be discouraged, could not be frightened away. From the simple demonstrations I had given with my laser gun, they had come to know the potential of the *Stardust*. They knew that to defy us was a risk so great that it was not worth taking. Even with the marvelous artifacts of the Sky People at their disposal, they knew that they had underestimated us.

This cavern vaulted high and spread wide. Even the biggest of the storage caves couldn't match it for size. A pattern of incandescent globes lit it brilliantly. And for the first time there were blue men in numbers.

I was instantly aware of the security precautions that the *Volloon* had set up. The cavern had a number of exits, and by each of these a small squad of grim blue knifemen clustered. As we strode in, the squad by our portal stepped back to let us pass. Then they blocked the way behind us.

"This is it," Pegleg said happily. He loves a showdown. "Do you really need both those lasers? Mine was borrowed, you remember."

I unstrapped the holster of my left-hand gun and handed it over. Pegleg buckled it on and shook it free to get the feel of it.

"A man does his best work with the proper tools," he murmured.

"You won't need it," I said. "This is all face-saving. If they had thought they could handle us, we wouldn't be here. This is a summit conference. Recognize the old boy out front?"

San had slowed his pace. He was walking now with a deliberate, dignified stride. His carved death's-head of a face had no expression, yet it projected an impression of implacable purpose. The chief was asserting his position. He was subservient to nobody.

There were perhaps twenty robed figures in the group waiting for us. One man, inordinately thin and tall, stood a stride in advance.

"It's old Bony," Pegleg said. "He's going to get his feelings hurt this time, for sure. Look at San!"

San had come to a halt perhaps three strides from the *Volloon*. He said no word. He simply stood there, cold, his face like stone, his bleak slits of eyes unwavering. He seemed to imply that talk wasn't necessary, that everyone knew what the problem was, and that it was the *Volloon*'s move.

Finally the robed man spoke, reluctantly, I thought.

"San!"

San let the tension build before he acknowledged, "Ben!"

The *Volloon* hesitated, wet his thin lips with a long blue tongue. He was on the defensive and he didn't quite know how to proceed. But I got another impression, too. He wasn't quitting. Many thousands of generations of tradition stood behind him. No man challenged the *Volloon*.

Ron had drifted back to us. He was dignified, too, but his speech made no attempt to hide his glee.

"Never thought I'd see this! I always knew old Ben wasn't big enough for his robe. I'll tell you what goes, Roscoe. If you want to give me the word, I'll pass it on."

"Right. Let's hear his position. I can say only that it had better be good."

I found my anger slowly rising again. That incredible old skeleton was the main thing that stood between me and Lindy. I gritted my teeth. Pegleg noticed.

"This is no time for muscles, Roscoe. I think we've won the war without shooting. Just a matter of time now, pal. Take it easy!"

"Right on!" Ron backed him up. "Take it easy!"

The *Volloon* began to speak, his tones high and positive.

"He says," Ron translated, "that you are not the Sky People. Your ship is wrong, and you do not know the words. You have no right to the treasures."

"Well, whoever said we were?" Pegleg looked his disgust. "We're just simple travelers, seeing the sights. We didn't even know this stuff was here. Remarkable it is, but piracy and thievery are out of our line!"

"Quiet," I said, "you're spoiling the broadcast!"

San spoke a short, high sentence, then added in his brand of English, "Lindy, *kantokar,* no!"

The *Volloon* answered with more high-pitched, emphatic talk. His features never changed, but he gestured violently with his bony arms. His long blue robe whipped.

"He says that the picture was not made from the woman.
She only pretends to be like it. She was taken to make sure
that you have no claim to the treasure."

San's answer again was short and to the point. Ron fairly
wriggled with pleasure. For some reason he had a special
prejudice against the *Volloon*.

"San says the *Volloon* have no right to collect people.
Release the women now, he says. He makes no bargains."

Even I could see that the old blue man was taking it hard.
As far back as memory ran, the *Volloon* had been a people
apart. They were the agents of the Sky People. No one
contested them. No one had ever given them an order. No one
had the right.

"Ron," I said, "tell San to say that we are a different Sky
People. We are much more powerful than the ones who left
the treasures. Say that we want only our women. Otherwise
we will have to destroy everything. Tell old Bony that."

I hope that's what Ron said. Knowing his bias, he may
have embroidered it a trifle.

San listened, flicked his cold slits of eyes at me, and
considered. Old Ben stood dignified and remote, but his
hands fidgeted. Then San spoke again.

He spoke slowly and his voice was deep, as when he tried
to speak English. Gone was the high Hadornian pitch.
probably wouldn't have recognized my original statements
after Ron changed them to suit himself, and now, I felt sure
San was adding his bit. He was issuing as plain an ultimatum
as I had ever heard, even though I couldn't understand a word
of it.

The *Volloon* said a few short words, evidently a question.

San answered at more length, still in those deep, deliberate
tones.

Ron chuckled. "San's tearing him down," he said. "The
Volloon will go on being the Keepers of the Treasure, but
they'll have to listen to the rest of us from now on. San is
telling him you will have to have a present—a big present—to
cool your anger. He's telling him he's lucky you don't run
flames through all his corridors and burn up everything that

lives. Oh,'' he listened a moment, ''he's saying you also want your gun back.''

''Bad idea,'' Pegleg muttered. ''It may remind him that he has a little potential himself. I'd hate to be held up with my own gun.''

''No problem,'' Ron said. ''He wouldn't risk it. He knows that there are many on your skyship.''

I wasn't diverted by all the conversation. I suspected that both Ron and Pegleg were talking partly to keep my impatience from building.

''We're skirting the point,'' I reminded them. ''What about the women? What about Lindy?''

The *Volloon* was speaking again. His high tones were softer, less emphatic, and he made placating gestures. Behind him the bank of robed figures could have been carved from the rock. At every entrance the lean knifemen listened in frozen silence. Only old Ben moved.

''He says,'' Ron relayed, ''that if you say you do not want the treasures, and will go away soon, the women will be released. He says''—Ron's slits of eyes looked at me a little dubiously—''he says that the woman of the picture has an injured foot, and must be transported by animal back. He says that he will be glad to have her go.''

My hand squeezed hard on the butt of my gun. In the bright glare of the cavern lights I could see only red. I was as immobile as the *Volloon*, for I didn't trust myself to move.

''Easy, Roscoe!'' Pegleg said soothingly. ''Lindy's okay. Let's hear the rest of it.''

''The Sky People would want you to have a large gift,'' Ron went on. ''The *Volloon* do not know what would please you, so you may choose from this room. Anything you can carry.''

San was standing with regal patience while Ron, as he said, 'gave us the word.'

''That old buzzard is crooked to the last,'' Pegleg growled. ''Anything we can carry, forsooth! It's a wonder he doesn't say anything we can carry down the cliffs. What'll we tell him, Roscoe?''

''Tell him,'' I ordered, ''that he will release the women

now. When they are free, we will discuss the matter of presents. Until they are free, the *Volloon* are in great danger, and the treasures could be destroyed.''

It was finally clear to us both that it was the artifacts that were important to these strange warped men. Without them, life would be meaningless to the *Volloon*. The treasures *were* their lives. When we understood this, our problem was no longer a problem.

Chapter 20

I didn't see the *Volloon* make a sign, but somehow the message had gone out. At the far end of the cavern a wide door slid into the wall. From the corridor beyond came a sound that I hadn't heard since I was a boy. It was familiar, but it had a character all its own. It was wild, ringing, and it seemed to carry a challenge to this whole blue world. It was the neigh of a stallion.

"Not just any old horse," Pegleg chuckled. "A man horse! Look! I told you your woman was okay."

The knifemen gave way at the portal. The stallion came charging through, his head flung high, mane whipping, and the mean light in his china-blue eyes could be seen the length of the cavern. He was a sleek slate-blue, his hide glistened, and his long tail almost touched the cavern floor.

Lindy rode him. She came sweeping down the main aisle like a rodeo queen, her red curls flying. She was laughing. Then she swung her mount in a zigzag pattern through and around the stacks of chests and cartons that filled the big room. The stallion's hooves drummed on the stone floor. His neigh pealed again, sounding almost like a scream. Lindy finally brought him to a quivering halt between San and the old leader of the *Volloon*.

We stared as she soothed and petted the horse, sliding her hand along his arching neck, talking softly to him.

"Steady, Blue Boy. Easy, fellow. You just eat hay, remember? You're not supposed to go around kicking the bejabbers out of people, no matter how much they need it. Quiet, boy!"

I've watched Lindy's creature magic on many words, and it still amazes me. She's everything's friend. The stallion subsided and stood still, but his evil blue eyes continued to

look at the whole scene with distrust. And his appearance was
not improved by the two fangs, evidently elaborated canines,
that curved downward and lay in grooves outside his lower
lip. Modern horses haven't got such structures. But this one
had.

Instinctively, Lindy knew what to do first. She knew that I
could see her, see that she wasn't harmed. So she turned
graciously to the blue chief.

"San!" she said, and held out her hand. "Friend!"

If San hadn't already been committed to Lindy's well-
being forever, that would have done it. His grim face softened, then slowly broke into the amazing smile she had
taught him.

"Lindy!" he said, and reached out his own mighty paw.
"F'iend!"

The stallion bared his teeth like a wolf. Lindy slapped him
lightly on his neck and snubbed the reins hard.

"Blue Boy, no!" she said sternly. The horse quieted
sulkily.

Then she looked across at me. She didn't have to say
anything. We communicate in ways nobody else can fathom.
We can be alone together in a crowd. So she said only,
"You're my friend too, Roscoe. You'll have to lift me off
Blue Boy, I'm afraid. I banged up a foot on the way into this
interesting place, and I guess I broke a bone. A little *Stardust*
magic will make it all better. Meanwhile, it hurts!"

I strode past the blue guard and held out my arms to my
woman. The stallion snarled at me, but I ignored him. It had
been a rough trip. These past days had tested me in ways I'd
never experienced before. But with that beautiful warm body
in my arms, it was as if they had never been.

I held her for a minute, just to convince myself that she was
real. And the way she squeezed me confirmed once more that
she was exactly where she wanted to be.

The injured foot, smoothly bound, was thrust out stiffly as
I held her. I felt a pulse of anger return.

"Who hurt you?" I growled. "And how?"

Her giggle pealed. In an instant she was everybody's Lindy
again.

"You sound like Blue Boy would, if he could talk. No one's to blame, Roscoe. I did it myself."

"Might I ask how?"

She attempted to move the foot and winced. Then she grinned, and winked a greeting to Pegleg over my shoulder.

"Serves me right, really. But you can imagine that I was a mite annoyed when those large blue gentlemen swooped down on us and packed us off without even asking if we wanted to go. I felt that their motives might be questionable. So the first time my man set me on my feet, I was ready. I gave him a karate kick that should have brought him down like the old pine tree."

She grimaced. "It was like kicking a mountain. He never changed expression, and the pain that went stabbing up my leg told me that I was out of the contest. After that he *had* to carry me. I guess they would have done that anyway, for they were in a bit of a hurry. We couldn't have traveled at their speed for five minutes."

She wriggled in my arms, so I set her gently on her feet—or rather, foot.

"I can stand," she said. "I just can't walk."

The stallion flung up his head and neighed piercingly. He was answered by a higher, thinner call. A dark-haired girl rode sedately under the arch through which Lindy had come charging on Blue Boy. Her mount was a plump blue mare which picked up its pace at the stallion's cry.

"That's Blue Boy's girlfriend," Lindy explained. "Barbara rides her. We've been keeping them together because his manners are pretty bad, and she has a soothing influence on him."

"A familiar story," I said. "My manners are improving already."

As she rode up the girl's dark eyes jumped eagerly from me to Pegleg, and then roamed with increasing disappointment over our backup group of tall slingmen.

"He's overhead, Barbara, in his scoutboat, ready to blast this plateau to bits if we don't bring you out in good shape. You'll just have to be glad to see us. We're the best we can do at the moment." Pegleg's sour drawl was gently derisive, but he knew that the little technician could hear the sympathy in it. Pegleg's more sentimental than he acts. When he wants to, he can charm a bird out of a bush.

"I'm sorry, Dr. Williams," the girl said. "I'm glad to see *anybody* who isn't tall and blue and skinny. But you don't blame me for hoping, do you?"

"Pete's okay, Barbara," I said. "He'd be here if he had a choice. But he knew he could help best as an eye overhead. You'll see him before too long."

The stallion whickered and touched noses with the mare. The girl slid lithely from the blue pad which was her saddle.

"What about them?" she asked. She barely motioned toward the unmoving cluster of robed figures.

"They've agreed to a truce. They made a mistake. They thought we had come to Hadorn to put them out of business."

Lindy leaned against me, supporting herself on her one good foot.

"Just the same," she said, "more than an apology is called for. Why us, anyway? We have suffered severe emotional trauma, not to mention one busted foot."

"It's a story best told aboard the *Stardust,* with your foot in a cast, and everybody rested again. Ron!"

"On the ball, Roscoe!"

Two pairs of eyes—one green, one dark—widened at the slingman's easy response.

"Tell San to tell old Bony that we have decided on the present we want. We don't want to carry anything away. As far as we're concerned, the *Volloon* can be caretakers of all this stuff forever. We have no right to interfere. But—" I looked sternly across at the old leader of the *Volloon,* then back to San's intent, inscrutable face, "we claim the right to look."

"A little more," Ron begged. "I can tell better if I know just what you want to see."

"Everything," I said. "Whatever the Sky People left. We have those aboard who know about each kind of thing. They must be allowed to come in and to see." I waved an arm at the long rows of bales and chests and boxes that filled the cavern. "This, I think, is a room of records. We have people who love records. They will look, but they will not harm. Make that clear.''

"Got it!''

Ron strode over to San, and the two strange giants conferred in their high speech. Then San addressed the *Volloon*. Anyone could tell that he was spelling out the law. And if he was being arrogant, I felt that that was excusable, under the circumstances. The provocation had been considerable. I watched the slow grin form on Ron's skeletal face as he listened. Ron had not only learned our speech, he was rapidly learning our habits as well.

"It's so nice we're not in a dull business," Lindy murmured. "I won't even ask how he learned to talk. I suppose it's another one of those stories best told back on the *Stardust*.''

"I have a smart wife," I said.

"You also have a wife whose feelings have been hurt. Roscoe, I *do* want to take something away from here.''

"An artifact?" I shook my head. "Too late. If old Bony goes along, I've given my word.''

"Not an artifact. A friend.''

I looked into those wide green eyes. Deep in them, as always, there was a devil dancing. Then I got it. I glanced at the stallion, which already had his distrustful, wicked blue eyes on me.

"Right," Lindy said. "I want Blue Boy.''

"Well," I hesitated, "he's certainly not an artifact. And I'll bet he doesn't have many other friends.''

"They'll let him go. They've got herds of them. And he's the orneriest of the lot. But he likes me, and he's big and smart. If he didn't hate you, you'd think he was beautiful.''

In a way, I suppose he was beautiful. He stood poised on slender legs, his long head flung high, his sleek neck arched. The ripple of blue mane along it glistened like silk, and so did his flowing tail. But there was the anomaly of the curved fangs. And when I looked at the stamping hooves, I did a double-take. On either side of every hoof was another toe, a splintlike toe that didn't quite touch the ground. A three-toed horse!

"An Earth horse, Roscoe," Pegleg spoke from behind me. "*Merychippus* grown tall. I don't know where the long teeth came from. Must have value in fighting. But his ancestors came with the Ramsgate people. He, too, is from Earth's Miocene."

Right then, I decided. "We'll have to take the mare, too. He'd be insufferable without her."

Ron looked down on us. "I have listened. You wish me to tell San that the women will accept the carrier beasts as a sign of friendship. Right?"

"On Earth," I said, "you could be elected to Congress. Tell him!"

The slingman studied me speculatively. He understood that it was a joke. All he lacked was the background. "Congress," he said thoughtfully. "Some kind of guiding group to which men are added by their friends. For their own benefit, I'd suspect. Well, what's wrong with that?" That last was another of Pegleg's favorite questions. Ron's slit eyes gleamed, and he turned to pass the information along to San.

The *Volloon* agreed to our terms. Not gracefully, but because they couldn't see that they had any other choice. This was my guess, prompted by Ron's gleeful asides. He delighted in the discomfort of the grim robed men.

And having signed the truce, so to speak, the *Volloon* didn't socialize. Their death's-head faces never changed as they turned and stalked away in a body, on out through the wide portal through which the girls had ridden. And around the cavern the squads of knifemen relaxed. They talked among themselves in soft high tones. But they didn't approach us. We had *carte blanche,* apparently. Equally apparently, we weren't going to get any help.

I think we all had but one idea: to get out of there and go home. We'd be back. Researchers in a dozen fields would call us blessed for this day's work. For weeks to come, crews from the *Stardust* would throng those corridors and caverns, photographing, recording, interpreting, speculating. And I knew that when they were finished, a new name would head the roster of Earth's historical geologists. Greater than Lyell. Greater than Leakey. Elias Ramsgate would be vindicated as a speculative scientist never had been before.

For me, there were other considerations as well. I was firm in my conviction that the blue men were of Earth origin. I knew it. As Ursula would say, couldn't say why. Had to be. But coming from me, that wasn't good enough. I only hoped that the anthropologists and geneticists and physiologists would find some supporting clues.

As the last blue robe disappeared through the portal, we turned to a more immediate problem. "I never thought that I'd welcome that miserable light outside," I remarked. "But nothing would please me better than to be out in it right now, headed back to the *Stardust,* a shower, a couple of eggs on toast, and a cup of coffee."

"Tea," Lindy substituted.

"Bourbon," Pegleg said, "but put it in a glass and don't dilute it with *anything.*"

I consulted Ron.

"We are ready to go back to our ship. Lindy's foot must be cared for, and we are tired. I suppose there are easier ways to get out of here than the way we came in."

The slingman didn't smile, but I felt his amusement. "There are many," he explained. "San will know. He is a leader, and has been shown. Not just anybody can come into the caverns of the *Volloon.* Most of our people have never seen the treasures. Unless a man can come up the cliff trail, he will not be regarded as fit."

"You dragged us up with ropes."

"Right enough, but you came the route. You weren't supposed to come anyway. We came up the cliff because it is our right. That way the entrance could not be closed to us."

"But you could have brought us an easier way?"

"There are openings at the bases of cliffs, where food is passed in, and others from which the rock pieces are carried out. But no person can go in there. The *Volloon* take the food; the outside workers take the rock chips and carry them away. It has always been like that."

"How about the carvings, the buildings in the big canyon? There are entrances there."

Ron's slit eyes looked down on me quizzically from the skull-face atop his skeletal frame.

"You don't miss much," he commented.

"A dish in the plateau five miles long and rimmed with great buildings is sort of hard to miss," I said.

"Suppose so. We've always been told that the Sky People could go through the air, but those scoutboats are something else. They bug San worse than anything else you do. That's how you found the Picture Buildings."

"Good try, but wrong. Pegleg stumbled on them. But the scoutboats make them easy to get to, and to study from the air."

Ron's face had no expression, but he rolled his eyes upward.

"What fitness is necessary to travel in one?"

"You have to know somebody," I said. "And you do. Me! When we get out of here, you've got a ride coming. Don't let me forget it."

"Don't worry, bub," Ron said.

San knew the way. As I suspected, the easiest and most accessible exits were into the amphitheater, the broad canyon of what Ron had called the Picture Buildings. After less than an hour of traveling through wide, brightly lighted corridors, we emerged through the main palace entrance into the blue world again.

The girls rode their horses, a blank-faced slingman at each bridle bit. And suddenly I wasn't tired anymore, and Pegleg strode along without a limp. When the great palace doors swung wide, we all stopped for a minute to look out over the carefully ordered and landscaped park, with its neatly trimmed vegetation and its maze of immaculate stone-chip trails. The blue sun was low.

Long blue shadows were already filling the valley, but the flickering fires of Bud Merani's archaeologists' camps glowed dull red through the gloom. High above, a single scoutboat swept in slow circles. We went down the wide, magnificent flight of granite steps, the horses picking their way gingerly, and then we were surrounded with good Earth faces, all with wide expressive grins and good intelligible shouts of welcome.

The scoutboat dropped down into the valley in a long slow glide. The pilot had a special interest in our little party. And it wasn't long before Lindy and Barbara were safely aboard and on their way back to the *Stardust*. Pete had rigged a bosun's chair for his boarding ladder, so that Lindy could swing on and be drawn up into the drifting ship.

Those forty kilometers of rocky trail seemed a bit much to Pegleg and me, too, and we gladly accepted a ride in the scoutboat sent to pick us up. San and Ron and the tireless slingmen would go home through the blue night, back to their shelters and their women on the bank of the cold Blue Danube. And they would bring the horses, and leave them at the *Stardust* in the morning.

Part III

Earth's First Sowing

Chapter 21

"Attention, all executive and advisory personnel! Dr. Rasmussen requests the pleasure of your company at dinner two days from this date, at 1800 hours. Be prompt and look pretty. There'll be local guests!"

That was a first for Stony Price, that announcement. Never before had natives of an alien planet attended a Rasmussen dinner. But at the first one on Hadorn, Johnny had given his word. He never forgot.

It had been four long Hadornian weeks since we had left the caverns of the *Volloon*. We were rested again. Lindy's foot had almost healed with appropriate care, and she was agile and busy on her light crutches. Blue Boy and his lady had been installed in proper quarters near Jim Peters's complex of enclosures and cages and tanks. Each day Lindy and the little technician rode them down a ramp and out for a run along a trail through the blue grain.

The *Stardust* was as nearly empty as it was ever allowed to get. Cap'n Jules Griffin had always implacably insisted that 10 percent of the ship's personnel be aboard at all times. Cap'n Jules did not change his mind now. He still insisted on it, so each discipline was forced to the making of duty rosters, to contribute its share to the minimum number of people manning the ship.

The attractions, of course, were the marvelous museums of the *Volloon,* the hundreds of caverns filled with the artifacts of the vanished Sky People. The trail into the valley of the Picture Buildings was used more in those four weeks than it had been for centuries. Jumper teams tapped and soared along its twisting length. Pegleg's jeep traveled it, not without some difficulty. And scoutboats glided down over

173

the valley, dropping off passengers and picking them up again with their trailing ladders.

I had given my word, and nothing was taken. But the cameras clicked endlessly, intricate energy analyses were made, the best specialists in the galaxy in every discipline murmured their notes, their observations and their speculations into recorders that automatically organized, classified and collated them. The artifacts would remain where they were, but we would be taking them with us just the same.

Ursula Potts came into the park via the jeep, not the first time Pegleg had had her for passenger. Since that time nine years ago, when she had ridden with us into Armageddon on Cyrene IV, Pegleg had often transported her. Those two strange geniuses had a wry respect for one another. Pegleg patiently loaded and unloaded canvases, sketch pads, paints, brushes, an easel, a camp stool, and the red umbrella that in this world would never show red. And Ursula sat in the park for the whole of a Hadornian week, sketching and painting the matchless carvings that were the buildings that rimmed the valley.

She did not work in her usual solitude. Of us all, none fascinated the blue men more than this little wizened woman with the pale eyes, who made pictures grow on her canvases that were in their way as marvelous as the art of the unknown Sky People. So while she dabbed away, an ever-shifting crowd of giant blue slingmen, skeletal faces inscrutable as always, watched with the cold intentness that they gave to everything.

Ursula ignored them. Yet I think it was their presence that must have inspired the painting that to me was the most significant of all, a painting not done in the pale light of the blue sun, but later, in the perfect illumination of her studio. It was the day of the dinner that she called me in to see.

"What do you think, Roscoe?"

I wonder how many times she has said that to me. Always when she says it, I look with attention. It means that her weird sixth sense is working, that an idea has come through, and has flowed along her skinny fingers onto the canvas before her. There on that canvas, if one can read it, is often the answer to a basic question; a problem we all have been grappling with. So I looked closely at what she had done.

It was a big canvas. At first it appeared somewhat pointless and confusing, that long line of small figures that marched across it, following a trail just faintly hinted at, winding through the features of a shadowy landscape. The background color, too, was strange. At the top of the picture the little men—for men they were—tramped along in a rosy glow. But as the trail twisted down across the canvas, the background paled, became cold, and a blue mist lay over hills and valleys almost watermarked against a pallid sky.

As they approached the bottom of the canvas the little men grew larger, more distinct, more familiar as they drew nearer to the viewer. And the last one, the one closest, seemed almost to stride out of the picture, although he was still no larger than my thumb. He was a blue man, a gaunt, skeletal, frozen-faced slingman, sling° on forearm, slender knife gleaming, all painted in exquisite detail. Only a great artist could have achieved that effect, for the picture was alive; the figures marched.

Then I realized that the first figure, too, the one that began the line at the top of the canvas, was depicted with the same minute completeness. Around him the rosy glow was strongest. And he wasn't a slingman at all. He wore intricate and colorful clothing, his luxuriant hair curled around his shoulders, and a pleasant smile was on his strong face. He was an Earthman. And he could have stepped from one of the paintings in the magnificent galleries of the *Volloon*.

I let my eyes go along the long line of tiny marching figures, winding and doubling back down through the misty landscape. Subtly, they changed. And there was no break in the line.

Slowly, I nodded my head. Of course! That was the way it had to be. Simple. Obvious.

"The *Volloon* can be at ease," I said. "The Sky People will never return."

"Makes sense, does it? Thought you'd see."

"Because they never went away!"

"Know it. Felt it all along. Had to be. Can't prove it, though."

"Neither can I. If we had time—years on this planet—we might. There may be something in the records that hint at the truth. There must be artifacts, remnants of intermediate stages of evolution. But whether we find them or not, there's no doubt in my mind. The blue men *are* the Sky People, strangely mutated by millions of years in this blue light.

"For some reason they could not, or didn't wish to leave, even when the light quality began to change. I hope Phil Julio will have some data on that. But they took apart their starships, carried their treasures deeper and deeper into the natural caverns of the plateau and range. They preserved everything. The more cavern spaces they dug and chiseled and carved, the better care they could take of their effects. It became a continuing and an endless task. They lived in the past. Their reason for being was short-circuited, so to speak. They lived to preserve their memories. And in preserving, they forgot."

"Double-talk," Ursula said. "I follow, though. Reason I called you in."

I turned my attention again to the brilliant, challenging painting, a painting geologic epochs long. That trail, with its unbroken line of tiny marching figures, wound through ten million years. I began to think aloud, almost as if Ursula were not there.

"They had to eat. They had brought with them needful life, animals in variety, many kinds of plant seeds. Some lived, many died. Most of the people spread out from the landing area, searched out and grew the food they needed. But they took nothing from the starships but the living things. For some reason, even then, everything had to be kept, to be preserved. And some of them watched and guarded and cared for the artifacts, and those outside fed them. They became a group apart, with a special mission—to preserve the treasure. They became—the *Volloon!*"

"Watchers," Ursula mused. "Keepers, guardians, defenders."

"Curators," I grinned. "I'll bet that's all the word means. We made an ominous meaning out of an unknown sound. I'll check it out with Ron."

"Remarkable man," Ursula said.

"Without a doubt," I agreed. "Sounds good, doesn't it Ursula? To be able to say 'man' and mean it?"

"Still one hurdle."

I considered. "I think I know—but name it."

"They evolved first, if we're right. Earth produced them millions of years before us. They first had the form, the intelligence, the adaptability. We had a different, a later origin. So—if they are men—what are we?"

It was a conundrum, a quibble. I could see the amusement in her pale eyes. It was an unprecedented phenomenon just the same. Parallel evolutions, strangely similar beings from worlds remote from each other—these we had seen. But to have a race uncannily like our own to precede us in our own environment—that was a new thought.

"What's a name, after all?" I said. "It only identifies, designates. It neither describes nor explains. The viewer, the student has to do that. *'Volloon'* doesn't repel me now, but when it represented an unknown menace, it did."

Ursula nodded.

"Didn't mean men exactly, did we? Meant Earth beings that were like us. Even erratic, like us. Why did they leave Earth, which seems good to us, and stay on here even after the light was reduced to blue?"

I shook my head. "There'll be many a debate. The thing that strikes me now is—we have come a hundred light-years to learn something about Earth; to confirm the speculations of a man who was thought to be at least maudlin, if not mad. Ramsgate *said* that the Earth had had two sowings; that these beings who have become the Blue Men were first; the second was the human race."

Chapter 22

I think we had never approached a Rasmussen dinner with quite the anticipation of this one. We knew that we were to have, not two guests, but four. It was through Ron that the dinner invitation had been extended to the chief and his impressive lady. And, since I knew him best, I had extended it. I had tried to explain to Ron this custom of ours, of gathering in a large group to take food together; but a time of talking as well as eating, a time to be friends together.

Ron understood. "There was a picture," he said, "a picture in the picture caverns of the *Volloon,* where many of the people sat along a single long board. The board was covered with bowls and dishes of food. Each person had a round trencher of his own, and a container for drink, and different knives and forks and small ladles. The people wore garments with much color, clean and not torn. All were smiling."

He eyed me, his skeletal face impassive, his cold slits of eyes reading my mind. "It is this custom your chief wishes San and Del to join?"

I knew at that moment that San and Del were not enough. I expanded Johnny's guest list on the spot, without consulting the host, and without a twinge of apprehension. I knew I was right. I nodded.

"San and Del and you and Mel. Four friends."

The big slingman tried to mask his delight, but it was no go. His cold face crinkled, broke, and he grinned. His acceptance was a key to the man. (Yes, I said *man!*)

"Mel will like," he said.

We cleared his understanding of the time of the dinner. And there was one thing more. He looked at my battered field garments, considerably the worse for wear. At that, I was more dressed than my custom was. The blue light of Hadorn was chill.

"You will wear other robes?" He didn't miss a trick.

"We'll probably spruce up a bit," I admitted. "Don't let it bother you, though."

"We will follow your custom," Ron said.

What that meant I didn't know, but I passed the conversation along to Johnny verbatim.

We found out, though.

I was watching, so I saw them coming from far off, four gaunt figures moving easily and swiftly through the blue grain. I knew that they were distance travelers, that the few miles from the village meant nothing to them. I had expected that they would come just that way. So I headed for the nearest personnel port to welcome and to bring them in.

Something made me pause. Maybe I've associated with Ursula so much that I've begun to share her weird sixth sense. Anyway, suddenly I knew that I shouldn't go out yet. Instead, I watched.

They stopped when they were perhaps no more than a hundred feet from the ship. Their still, expressionless faces revealed nothing as each unrolled a bundle carried under a skeletal arm. They were wearing breech coverings and sheath knives, as usual. But almost in seconds they changed. With movements almost as facile as the swift wrapping of sling around arm, each shook out a glinting blue robe and draped it over bony shoulders. Then each turned slowly in place, apparently checking the hang and fit of the garment.

Then solemnly, two by two, the tall robed figures walked slowly, with immense dignity, toward the personnel port. They had dressed for the party under the eyes of half the *Stardust* crew, and it hadn't taken them half a minute.

I checked that against the shaving, the showering, the grooming that I had just subjected myself to, up to and including the tying of that blasted black tie. That always takes me ten minutes. And my beautiful wife had sat long before her dressing table, doing all the mysterious things she does to gild the lily. So I wondered, wryly, who the barbarians really were.

"Ladies and gentlemen, good evening!"

Johnny Rasmussen was a tall man, and the sleek perfection of his grooming, his grave, lean face with moustaches waxed to points, always made him seem taller. But for once his guests overshadowed him. He bowed graciously, but he had to look up at the Hadornians' looming height. Still, he didn't change his custom. Looking to his right, he named names.

"San, Dr. Kissinger, Del, Dr. Peterson—" On around the long curved table he went, concluding with "Miss Potts, Mel, Dr. Williams, Ron," as he got back to himself. Of course, that alignment had to be the way of it. We were the Earth folk who knew the blue people best. For all that, I hadn't expected them to be in the least awed by the situation—and they weren't.

"I am delighted to have you here this evening. It is especially gratifying to welcome our friends of Hadorn. Won't you please be seated?"

Johnny had made every adjustment. The section of table before each of the blue people had been raised to their tolerance; the chairs were crafted to their dimensions. They sat when we sat, gathering the blue robes about them with a smooth grace I'd never have suspected. Four pairs of blue slits of eyes watched our movements with unwinking attention. They did what we did, and not once did they even pick up a wrong piece of silver.

That should have been the most awkward, the tensest meal we ever ate. But to my growing astonishment, it wasn't at all. It was almost as if the blue people were hosts. They looked cold and enigmatic, but they were completely at ease.

And they socialized. We spoke to each other with smiles on our faces. Soon the grim, skeletal visages of our guests softened, and they smiled when we smiled.

They talked, too.

For Ron, of course, there would never be another opportunity like it. Conversationally, he was the Hadornian equivalent of Pegleg. And since most of his English phrasing had come from that source, the resemblance was marked, and somewhat ludicrous. But he had the words, he knew their meanings, and he coordinated the talk around him with complete confidence, switching from interpreter to commentator so effectively that we all seemed to be speaking the same tongue. That's harder than it sounds. Try it sometime.

"The *Volloon* should see," Ron said, his slits of eyes sweeping the colorful company down the long curved table. "For them the Sky People have never had life. The pictures are only pictures. The things of the starships have no uses. This is real!" He waved a great hand.

"They would be welcome to come and see," Johnny Rasmussen said. "Would they come?"

Ron spoke to Del, a high-pitched, flowing sentence. She turned her impressive blue face toward Johnny. The clean planes softened slightly, the narrow eyes crinkled. Very slowly she shook her head. It was a completely human gesture.

"No way," said Ron. "Del knows. Old Ben is her father's father."

"That puzzles us, Ron," I said. "If she is *Volloon,* why did she leave the caverns? Why would it be allowed?"

Ron grinned like Pegleg.

"She saw a man," he said. "A big man. Strong. One who gave orders. So she spoke to him from the portals each time he brought meat. And he saw a woman he liked."

"Now there, Roscoe, is the synopsis of a pretty familiar story." Pegleg looked across the table from Del to San, admiringly, I think. They smiled back, knowing that they were the topic, and confident that something good was being said. "Answers your question, too, I think. Who'd stop either one of them?"

When the meal began, the fifty or more people around the long table were quiet, restrained, covertly watching the strange blue people. But by the time the meat arrived, luscious broiled *vada* steaks from the planet Gossoon, the clatter of utensils and the rumble of conversation had reached their usual volume. It was again a Rasmussen dinner. The discussion topics ranged from field problems to speculation of blue-man origin. As always, nothing was sacred.

There was one lack. No one mentioned it, but all certainly noticed, for it had never happened before. With the sizzling steaks there was no red wine; no Chablis with the fish. When the meal had reached its end, and coffee arrived in large, fragrant cups, it had to stand on its own merits. There was no brandy to support it. No alcohol. The chief thinks of everything.

Rasmussen felt that even the coffee had to be explained.

"This is a drink from our world," he said to Ron. "It will be strange and may not please you. Say to San and Del and Mel that if the taste is not good, it is courtesy to leave it. Some never learn to like it."

Ron spoke briefly in the high Hadornian accents. Each of the blue people sipped cautiously at the steaming cups, barely moistening their thin lips. Then, to my considerable amusement, they let the cups sit untouched. I decided to go along. A guest should feel at ease. So I resisted the fragrant odor, and let my own cup cool in front of me.

For once, Rasmussen made no speech. At the proper moment he simply rose, bowed slightly as he usually did.

"It has been a pleasure to have you here this evening. Dr. Kissinger, Dr. Peterson and Dr. Williams will show our guests the *Stardust*. They will then return to Main, where Miss Potts will have a painting that will summarize all we know or suspect of the origin of the people of Hadorn. And there will be additional refreshment for those who would like it. Orange juice! Good evening!"

Our guests were gone.

They had viewed the wonders of the *Stardust* with the same intentness, the same implacable concentration that was always the most striking feature of the blue-man personality. And I noticed that, as we led them from shops to laboratories to living quarters, from the communications center to the record banks, from Cap'n Jules and Moe Cheng sitting in their accustomed places in Control to the scoutboats resting in their cradles, that the mobility of their blue faces gradually vanished. Their visages became again remote, expressionless and still.

I think we understood. After all, the changing expressions, the reflections of emotion and thought by lip-spreading, eye movement, relaxing and tightening of facial muscles—these were our customs, not theirs. The habits developed over millennia were not to be discarded overnight. Perhaps it was not necessary for man's thoughts and feelings to show on his face. Perhaps it was not even good. I reflected on those things as we watched the intent, unreadable, yet somehow infinitely dignified blue faces, the slit eyes fixing with complete concentration on each new wonder. I remembered how often we used our own faces to dissemble; how readily our lips smiled when we were not smiling inside. The carved features of our blue guests told no lies; they told nothing at all.

It was almost the same when they said good-bye. They had stalked solemnly from group to group in Main, offering their great, well-shaped hands and intoning, gravely, 'F'iend.' For this ritual, even Ron reverted. He spoke and behaved exactly like the others, even leaving the 'r' out of 'friend.' And I felt that it was not a final expression of the puckish humor we had come to know so well. It was a serious farewell, a blue-man farewell.

They knew that we were soon to go. For many thousands of years they had believed in and lived with a legend, with the story of the Sky People. And now we, Sky People certainly, had come, more marvelous than the legend. As Ron had said, we were *real.*

I tried to explain what we speculated to be the story of their Sky People. They had all looked long at Ursula's painting, their still faces revealing nothing of the wonder, the confusion, perhaps even the disbelief that was rolling around behind those changeless facades.

I think Ron understood. Whether or not he believed, I'll never know.

One thing I do know. Our fellow Earth people really meant their final words. Predecessors, relatives, whatever they were, they understood the meaning of 'f'iend.' We had tried to be as helpful, as noninterfering, as respecting of their lives and customs as they would have expected of the Sky People of their legend. We had changed their lives, changed their thinking, but we hadn't physically interfered. They appreciated that. Only the *Volloon* may have felt that it would have been better if we had never come. We could hope only that they were wrong.

We had gone with our guests, Lindy and Pegleg and I, to the exit portal when the evening was over. For a few minutes we stood together in the blue night, the three strange moons almost overhead in their tandem march across the cold sky. It was, for a brief time, a wordless leavetaking, regretted by us all. Then San shrugged the robe from his wide shoulders, folded and tucked it under a long arm. The others followed suit.

The tall chief looked down on my wife and, even in the blue moonlight, I could see his slit eyes soften. I knew he would never forget this Earth woman who was always happy; this woman who taught him to smile.

"Lindy," San said deeply, "good-bye!"

She smiled now, with tears rolling down her cheeks. She grasped his great hand with both of hers.

"Good-bye, San!" she said. "No matter what any evidence shows, you really are a man!"

We knew that the chief didn't understand the words, but he felt what lay behind them. He faced us all.

"Lindy, Osco, Pe-leg. Sky People. F'iend!"

Abruptly he turned and strode away into the blue grain.

With dignity the chief's stately lady offered her hand to each of us in turn, wordlessly. Then seemingly we ceased to exist as she followed her lord with long strides.

"Ron," I said, "you know the words. Tell your people about themselves, about us and about Earth. Tell them that they are as great a wonder to us as we are to them. Tell them that we believe that we all had the same home."

"I got the words, Roscoe," the slingman said. "I'll tell 'em."

Lindy held out her hand to Mel. Seven feet tall, skinny, cadaverous, somehow the blue woman looked like a shy girl. Her smile was there again, tremulous, genuinely sorrowful.

"And please tell Mel," Lindy said, "that she's beautiful."

"She knows it," the big slingman said. "I tell her all the time."

That was our last real contact with the blue people of Hadorn. Oh, we saw them, in the distance, in passing, even close at hand those last days as we worked and hurried back and forth in the caverns and corridors of the *Volloon*.

For one more Hadornian week we recorded, photo-graphed, duplicated and interpreted the treasures of the Sky People. And always we kept the word I had given. Nothing was taken. No tiny item was left misplaced. Grimly, inscru-tably, and I suspect, resentfully, the *Volloon* were always present, always watching, shadowy robed figures that seemed almost ghostlike, and somehow, forlorn. It must have been rough to become ordinary citizens, just museum keepers, after millennia as the Chosen of the Sky People.

We didn't finish. We never do. We couldn't. The *Stardust* is an explorer ship. Her function is to discover the inhabited worlds of the galaxy; to locate, to map and to describe. Regularly we return to our home slip at Tycho Base on Earth's Moon, to report, to refit and renew ourselves, to leave the wonders we have found to the generations of scholars who will study and interpret and ask the questions to be answered by the greater vessels that, sooner or later, will follow the *Stardust*'s trails.

So finally, on a cold blue morning, our big explorer-home began to run through its liftoff checklists. While it had lain there the grain around it had ripened, and we had watched the amazing harvest. The entire population of each village had swarmed into the grain. All of each day and into the blue nights the grain carts had plied back and forth.

There had been no sophisticated harvesting machines, no strange and wonderful ways of reaping what had grown with seemingly no attention at all. A curved knife flickering in each left hand, skillfully lopping the heads of grain, and the right hand catching and tossing them into the nearest cart. Tall teen-agers, women, men—they all worked at the same tireless, almost effortless pace.

We're not sure what was done with the grain. We were not invited to the harvest. And when we wandered out among the workers, we were ignored. We could have been rocks or trees. So we took the hint and watched from afar and from drifting scoutboats overhead. In her studio extruded through the hide of the *Stardust,* Ursula sat and painted as the flood of carts and swarming skeletal figures rolled slowly past, and finally faded into the blue distance.

And shortly after, our big ship lifted soundlessly.

The blue plains and brushy lands and the strange metallic glint of forests slipped along underneath as we made a last great sweep. The blue thread of the Danube showed, and the dwindling cluster of tiny shelters that was San's village. And I almost imagined that I could see the tall chief himself, striding out into an open space and raising a long, skeletal arm, while the marvelous ship of we real Sky People grew smaller and smaller in the cold blue sky.

We'll never find a planet with a stranger story, or one more meaningful to us. But it was a cold world. Not in temperature, but in feel. After all, we were people of a warm, a yellow sun. In all our stay there we were never cheerful for long, never ourselves. It was a depressing world, a blue-mood world. We were glad to leave.

But I have a picture on my laboratory wall, a picture in many shades of blue—one of the monitoring pictures that the *Stardust* takes automatically when any life is near it. A blue Lindy, blue lollipop in her hand, is standing, head tilted, looking up at a great, tall, cadaverous blue man—and they are laughing.

It looks right. Whether or not he's laughing still, he is doubtless happy in his blue world; a man totally unfitted for the brighter colors of the spectrum.

And Lindy is happy back where she belongs.

With me.